As soon as Mitch answered the phone, he knew it was trouble.

The voice was garbled, so that it was difficult to identify the gender of the caller. It could be a wrong number, but after years with the Bureau it was hard to ignore the uneasiness rising in his gut. He tried to avoid Terry's eyes. No use worrying her yet.

"Hello?" he said for the second time.

"Look in the dresser," the voice said.

"Who is this?" he asked, and Terry clutched his arm.

"Do it. Hope's dresser. Top drawer."

Fear exploded like an atomic bomb. This couldn't be happening. Not to him. He'd worked cases like this. Kidnappings were other people's nightmares.

The caller's evil laugh grated in his ear, and then there was a click.

"Hello?" Mitch threw the phone across the room, then ran to Hope's room with Terry right behind him. He yanked the top drawer so hard it left its tracks and crashed to the floor. He saw the note lying on top of Hope's pink sleeper.

In bold black letters were the words "DON'T CALL THE COPS—OR SHE DIES."

Dear Reader,

What fun it's been for me to be included in this exciting series. Since this is the last book, by now you all know the wonderful and sometimes devious but always exciting and compelling characters of Trueblood.

Terry and Mitch and baby Hope Katherine are of course special to me. May you enjoy their dreams and conflicts and lives as much as I did exploring them.

Well, it's back to work for me. A bunch of us authors have recently met the folks of Cooper's Corner— another new series we're all sure to enjoy. But, holy cow, do these people have their problems....

Debbi Rawlins

TRUEBLOOD, TEXAS

Debbi Rawlins

A Family at Last

HARLEQUIN®

TORONTO • NEW YORK • LONDON
AMSTERDAM • PARIS • SYDNEY • HAMBURG
STOCKHOLM • ATHENS • TOKYO • MILAN • MADRID
PRAGUE • WARSAW • BUDAPEST • AUCKLAND

Deborah Quattrone is acknowledged
as the author of this work.

Thanks, Marsha,
for your confidence and support. You're terrific!

HARLEQUIN BOOKS
225 Duncan Mill Road, Don Mills,
Ontario, Canada M3B 3K9

ISBN 0-373-65093-0

A FAMILY AT LAST

Visit us at www.eHarlequin.com

Printed in U.S.A.

TRUEBLOOD, TEXAS

THE TRUEBLOOD LEGACY

THE YEAR WAS 1918, and the Great War in Europe still raged, but Esau Porter was heading home to Texas.

The young sergeant arrived at his parents' ranch northwest of San Antonio on a Sunday night, only the celebration didn't go off as planned. Most of the townsfolk of Carmelita had come out to welcome Esau home, but when they saw the sorry condition of the boy, they gave their respects quickly and left.

The fever got so bad so fast that Mrs. Porter hardly knew what to do. By Monday night, before the doctor from San Antonio made it into town, Esau was dead.

The Porter family grieved. How could their son have survived the German peril, only to burn up and die in his own bed? It wasn't much of a surprise when Mrs. Porter took to her bed on Wednesday. But it was a hell of a shock when half the residents of Carmelita came down with the horrible illness. House after house was hit by death, and all the townspeople could do was pray for salvation.

None came. By the end of the year, over one hundred souls had perished. The influenza virus took those in the prime of life, leaving behind an unprecedented number of orphans. And the virus knew no boundaries. By the time the threat had passed, more than thirty-seven million people had succumbed worldwide.

But in one house, there was still hope.

Isabella Trueblood had come to Carmelita in the late 1800s with her father, blacksmith Saul Trueblood, and her mother, Teresa Collier Trueblood. The family had traveled from Indiana, leaving their Quaker roots behind.

Young Isabella grew up to be an intelligent woman who had a gift for healing and storytelling. Her dreams centered on the boy next door, Foster Carter, the son of Chester and Grace.

Just before the bad times came in 1918, Foster asked Isabella to be his wife, and the future of the Carter spread was secured. It was a happy union, and the future looked bright for the young couple.

Two years later, not one of their relatives was alive. How the young couple had survived was a miracle. And during the epidemic, Isabella and Foster had taken in more than twenty-two orphaned children from all over the county. They fed them, clothed them, taught them as if they were blood kin.

Then Isabella became pregnant, but there were complications. Love for her handsome son, Josiah, born in 1920, wasn't enough to stop her from growing weaker by the day. Knowing she couldn't leave her husband to tend to all the children if she died, she set out to find families for each one of her orphaned charges.

And so the Trueblood Foundation was born. Named in memory of Isabella's parents, it would become famous all over Texas. Some of the orphaned children went to strangers, but many were reunited with their families. After reading notices in newspapers and church bulletins, aunts, uncles, cousins and grandparents rushed to Carmelita to find the young ones they'd given up for dead.

Toward the end of Isabella's life, she'd brought together more than thirty families, and not just her orphans. Many others, old and young, made their way to her doorstep, and Isabella turned no one away.

At her death, the town's name was changed to Trueblood, in her honor. For years to come, her simple grave was adorned with flowers on the anniversary of her death, grateful tokens of appreciation from the families she had brought together.

Isabella's son, Josiah, grew into a fine rancher and married Rebecca Montgomery in 1938. They had a daughter, Elizabeth Trueblood Carter, in 1940. Elizabeth married her neighbor William Garrett in 1965, and gave birth to twins Lily and Dylan in 1971, and daughter Ashley a few years later. Home was the Double G ranch, about ten miles from Trueblood proper, and the Garrett children grew up listening to stories of their famous great-grandmother, Isabella. Because they were Truebloods, they knew that they, too, had a sacred duty to carry on the tradition passed down to them: finding lost souls and reuniting loved ones.

CHAPTER ONE

"WE'VE FOUND HER."

Mitch Barnes tightened his hold on the cell phone. "Where?"

"Here in San Antonio."

That surprised him. He figured she'd be long gone by now. Taking in a slow, steadying breath, he left the kitchen to look at Hope, asleep in her crib. "What now?"

On the other end, Lily hesitated. "I was going to ask you that."

"Right." Mitch closed his eyes and rubbed the back of his neck. It had been a few months since he'd hired Lily Garrett Bishop and her brother Dylan of Finders Keepers to locate Terry Monteverde. You'd think he'd be prepared to face her by now. "Where did you find her?"

"She's working at the Menger Hotel."

"Working?" Mitch frowned. "Doing what?"

"She's a maid."

Terry, heiress to All That Glitters, working as a maid? "Are you sure she's—"

"I'm sure. And, Mitch…" Lily cleared her throat. "I think you're right. I got a good look at her. She's got to be Hope's mother."

His gut tightened as he stared at his sleeping daughter. At eight months, her lashes were already thick and black, lying against soft olive-skinned cheeks. She was a real beauty. Apparently just like her mother.

Mitch tried not to wonder about what Terry looked like. Bad enough he could still remember that miraculous night in Rio, the way her silky chestnut hair had lain across his bare chest, the wicked things she'd done with her feather mask. But this wasn't about him. If it were, he wouldn't have bothered trying to find her. But he figured his daughter had the right to know why she'd been abandoned.

He couldn't tear his gaze away from Hope, still amazed at how much the child had become a major part of his life, how quickly they'd bonded. Terry had no idea what she'd given up. Even if she did, it was too late. Hope was his now.

"Mitch?"

"Yeah, Lily. I'm here." Weary suddenly, he scrubbed at his face. "Hope's nanny is out for another half hour. Can we meet once Margaret gets back?"

"Sure. Want me to pick you up?"

"No, I'll meet you in the parking lot of the Menger."

"Okay," she said slowly. "You know, Mitch, I doubt Terry is going anywhere. Maybe you ought to wait until tomorrow and think about how you'd like to approach her."

He wanted to laugh. As if he'd been able to think about anything else. Especially after screwing up his Achilles tendon and having to sit on his ass these past few months. The FBI had had no use for an agent who could barely hobble. And a man could do a hell of a lot of thinking when he wasn't in motion.

"Nothing's going to change between now and tomorrow. I don't need you to come along if—"

"I'll be there. Let's touch base again when Margaret gets home."

Mitch was about to agree when he heard a noise at the door. "Hold on, I think that might be her now."

He pulled Hope's door partially closed as he walked toward the foyer, pleased that he barely limped anymore. Margaret was already crossing the threshold when he got there. Her windblown hair frizzed around her shiny flushed face, and her arms were loaded down with two large grocery sacks. She smiled as soon as she saw him.

"Oh, Mr. Barnes, would you mind getting the door?"

"Let me call you back," he told Lily, then disconnected and stuck his cell in his pocket.

"I'm sorry. I didn't know you were on the phone."

"No problem. How about I take these, instead?" He lifted one of the sacks away from her. It wasn't very heavy but she was a small woman with barely enough meat on her bones.

"Thank you," she said, passing him the second bag, and blushing all the way to her hairline when he accidentally brushed the side of her breast.

He started to murmur an apology, but figured that would just make it worse. According to her résumé, she was in her early thirties but she seemed much older. Probably because she was so conservative, kind of old-fashioned.

But he'd been damn lucky to find Margaret. She'd been the first person the agency sent over, and he knew immediately she was the one. Efficient and always pleasant, she treated Hope as though she were her own child. She'd also been an enormous help in getting them settled in the new home he'd bought. If she had a fault, it was that she spent too much time fussing over him and Hope instead of enjoying a social life. Lily suspected Margaret had a thing for him. He didn't believe it.

"Look, I've got to run out for a while." He deposited the sacks on the kitchen counter. "I'm not sure how long I'll be, but if you have to leave—"

"Don't worry." Margaret waved a dismissive hand. "I have no plans this evening. I'll stay as long as you like."

"Thanks." He smiled, and she blushed again. "Want help unloading the groceries?"

"Well…" She shook her head, but her tone wasn't exactly convincing. "No, go ahead. You have other things to do."

He wasn't about to argue. He was so damn distracted with the knowledge he'd be seeing Terry again, he couldn't think about much else. "I have to make a quick call, and then I'll be leaving."

Her brows arched with curiosity, then she looked away. But not before he caught the flash of annoyance in her eyes. "Should I make dinner?"

"No." He headed toward the privacy of his study, already distracted again. "Thanks. Order something delivered if you want. There's cash in the junk drawer."

"Fine."

At the shortness in her tone, he glanced back, but she was busy unloading the grocery sacks. It wasn't like her to be abrupt, but he had too much on his mind to worry about it. Hell, everyone was entitled to a bad day.

Lily answered on the second ring, and they agreed to meet in the hotel parking lot in half an hour. That gave him an extra five minutes to sit and think. As if he didn't have enough time to do that these days.

It wasn't that he regretted his decision to leave the Bureau. He'd been a good agent, and through the FBI he'd finally figured out what kind of man he was— one he'd become pretty damn proud of. Growing up without a father had had its rocky times, and Mitch hadn't been the model son to his struggling single mother.

He'd had too many questions she wouldn't answer, some answers he couldn't accept. As a youth he'd rebelled, as an adult he was trying his best to do the right thing. That's why he had to talk to Terry. When Hope had questions about her absent mother, he'd have the answers.

Rotating his neck, working out the tension starting to build at his nape, he pulled out the Polaroid picture of her. It had faded some, but then it had been around, to Rio and back to Texas with the two men Dylan and Lily had hired to help with the case. Still, it had been enough to finally identify and locate Terry.

It wasn't going to be easy seeing her again. Even

after a year and a half. He'd been on assignment in Rio during Mardi Gras when they met in the garden behind the Perez mansion. Inside, the party had gotten too rowdy so he'd sneaked out for some air and saw her sitting alone on a white stone bench.

She'd asked him for a cigarette, and when he told her he didn't smoke, she laughed softly, and in that slight lilting accent said that was good, because she'd quit two years ago.

They'd talked nonstop for over three hours. She'd learned more about Mitch than any human being should know. And he'd been pretty sure he'd discovered what made Terry Monteverde tick.

Or so he'd thought. Hard to believe she was an embezzler and a diamond smuggler.

He glanced at the clock, and then slipped her picture back into his desk drawer. He was about to leave when he remembered to cancel tomorrow morning's appointment with his physical therapist. After looking up the number, he used his cell phone on his way out. He opened his study door and nearly ran into Margaret.

Surprise and annoyance flashed in her eyes. They disappeared just as quickly, replaced by a feeble smile as she took a step back.

Uneasiness bunched the muscles in his shoulders. Had she been trying to listen? "Did you want something?"

"No, not really." She shrugged, swiped at her frizzy hair. "You seemed upset earlier. Is there anything I can do to help?"

Mitch cursed to himself as she laid a tentative hand

on his arm. Maybe Lily was right. Maybe he'd been a fool not to see that Margaret acted more concerned than an employee should.

On the other end of the line, the receptionist answered, allowing him to disengage himself from Margaret's touch without being too obvious. He gave her a quick smile and turned his attention to his phone conversation while he dug car keys out of his pocket, and then headed toward the door to the garage as he wrapped up the call.

"Mitch?"

He turned, mildly surprised she'd used his first name. Something she normally refused to do.

"Are you sure you wouldn't like me to cook dinner?" She shrugged again, looking slightly embarrassed. "You know, maybe something a little special."

He frowned. "What's going on, Margaret?"

Her color heightened. "I don't mean to be nosy, but I'm guessing you found Hope's mother?" Margaret clasped her hands together tightly when Mitch didn't answer. "So I thought you might want to have a special meal waiting."

He'd never discussed his search for Terry with the woman, and he wasn't happy she'd been eavesdropping. "That won't be necessary."

"Okay." Her voice sounded small, and he noticed her hand shook when she pushed back her hair. "I'm sorry if I overstepped my bounds."

"Margaret?" A thought occurred to Mitch and he stopped her as she turned away. "Don't worry. Your job here is secure."

Her mouth curved with relief. "Thank you."

He gave her a brief, reassuring smile but said nothing more as he left the house. His thoughts had already returned to Terry. As much as he hated the fact she'd abandoned Hope, or the assurance that he was a man worthy of being the girl's father, he still couldn't let go of the night they'd made love.

She'd been the perfect woman to him—sensitive, giving, caring. When she'd talked about how impossible it was to please her father, the pain in her voice she tried to flippantly conceal was like a knife in Mitch's gut. Made him think twice about mourning the absence of his own father, and stirred a protectiveness toward Terry that overwhelmed him.

Of course, he knew better now. She wasn't the brave, but wounded, woman he'd thought she was. Accusations of smuggling, embezzlement and faking her own death still hung over her head. But her greatest crime, to Mitch's way of thinking, had been abandoning her baby.

And damn it, he couldn't stop wanting her.

It wasn't just the sex, no matter how incredible it had been, and not even the fact that they shared a child, but something had happened to Mitch that night. He'd stopped running long enough to listen, to be human, to give a damn about another person.

Caught up in his thoughts, he nearly missed the entrance to the hotel parking lot. Scary that he had no memory of even driving this far. His concentration was shot to hell. But that's the kind of stuff Terry had done to him. Or at least the memories he had of her. Pulling into a stall, he hoped to God those memories were inflated.

Lily was already waiting and she got out of her car as soon as she saw him. "This is actually good timing," she said, flipping back her long black hair. "Terry should be getting off work any minute. Yesterday she crossed the parking lot on her way to the bus stop. Let's hope that's her usual routine."

Mitch shot Lily a curious look. He'd assumed they had just found Terry today. But Lily was shading her eyes against the sun, busy scanning the parking lot, and he decided to let the matter drop. The important thing was that he was about to confront Terry.

The reminder brought dampness to his palms, the back of his neck. He'd stared into the barrel of a .45 twice and it hadn't made him this nervous. For Hope's sake, he had to pull himself together. This was about her. Only her.

"Mitch."

His gaze immediately went to Lily, who gestured with her chin to an area across the parking lot. He saw nothing but rows of nondescript cars at first, an older lady talking to a small redheaded child next to a faded blue sedan.

And then he saw her.

Terry's thick glossy chestnut hair stole the sunlight. And his breath. No matter that he'd never seen her face in daylight, or that her hair was much shorter now, Mitch would have known her anywhere. It was the graceful, sensual way she moved, her hips swaying to a silent but seductive rhythm. Her back was straight, her chin held up proudly, like a woman who knew exactly what she wanted. And how to get it.

Yet there was a softness about her, too, a fragility that her eyes couldn't quite conceal. The look had haunted Mitch for the past year and a half. It made him go soft inside.

Damn it. He couldn't afford soft. Not when this was about Hope.

He headed in Terry's direction, careful not to move too fast and spook her. The last thing he needed was to have to chase her with his bum leg.

Fortunately, she didn't seem to be in a hurry, slowing to raise her face to the warm breeze that had suddenly picked up. She lifted the hair off the back of her neck, and then let it go again. It shimmered like a blanket of satin as it settled almost to her shoulders.

Mitch swallowed. "Terry?"

She froze.

"Teresa Monteverde?"

Her entire body tensed and she looked poised for flight, but he knew she couldn't get far trapped between him and the silver Cadillac. Slowly she turned to him, her almond-shaped eyes full of panic. Recognition. Fear. Defeat.

"What are you doing here? How did you find—" Her frightened gaze flew across the parking lot. She started shaking her head. "This is dangerous. You don't understand—" Abruptly, she looked back at him. "Is she okay?"

There was so much fear in her face, her voice

shaky, nearly inaudible, that Mitch bit back the sarcastic retort that sprang to mind. "She's fine."

Her expression turned to relief and she teetered a little. "Thank God."

He reached for her, then thought better of it when his entire body hungrily reacted to the idea of touching her.

She straightened, and with an unsteady hand smoothed back her hair. It was much shorter. She'd whacked a good eight inches off since he'd last seen her. Or maybe his memory wasn't so hot, after all.

Their gazes met again, and her expression was now one of defeat. A mask of composure slid into place as she lifted her chin. "How did you find me?"

He didn't answer, but tried to steel himself against the way her soft lilting accent wrapped itself around his body. "We need to talk."

"Of course." She nodded and swept another nervous glance around the parking lot, this time settling warily on Lily.

"She's with me."

Terry's startled gaze flew back to Mitch. "Your wife?"

He shook his head. "One of the detectives I hired to find you."

She blinked, and the relief that briefly lit her face shouldn't have gotten to Mitch.

But it did. He shoved his hands roughly into his jeans pocket. "There's a coffee shop around the corner where we can talk."

"I know the place. I'll meet you there."

"No way." He grabbed her arm when she started

to turn away. Warm, smooth, her skin was as soft as silk. "We go together."

"I won't run from you, Mitch."

"Right."

Terry stared down at her feet and gingerly pulled away from him. It was obvious she knew he was thinking about the night they met. How between tangled sheets they'd shared secrets until dawn, and then she was gone. Without even a note.

"I don't have a car." She looked up at him, but he couldn't meet her eyes.

If he did, he'd be in trouble. She seemed so much smaller than he remembered...vulnerable. Of course she wasn't, he reminded himself. She was a woman capable of giving her own child away to a virtual stranger. "I have mine."

She sighed. "We shouldn't be seen together, Mitch. It's not safe."

"Nice try. Let's go." He took her arm again, ignoring her when she tried to jerk free.

"You don't understand. It's Katherine I'm worried about."

"Katherine?"

"Our daughter...we can't afford to let anyone make the connection between you and me. There's this man—" She waved an agitated hand, mumbled something in Portuguese. "You'll lead him back to her."

"You mean Leo Hayes?"

She went still, only her eyes widening with absolute terror, and he knew he'd made a mistake. He should have told her right away.

"He's dead, Terry. Hayes is dead."

"Oh, my God." Her gaze became unfocused and she slumped in Mitch's arms.

CHAPTER TWO

MITCH'S HAND tangled in her hair as he cradled her to his chest. He rubbed her back, breathed in the clean vanilla scent of her smooth olive skin. "It's okay," he whispered. "Hayes won't bother you anymore."

Her breaths came in three deep shudders. She sagged against him for another second, and then straightened, her hands lingering on his chest as she stared up at him. "When?"

"It's been at least a month."

"Are you certain?"

The desperation in her voice tore at him. But it wasn't over, he reminded himself, not by a long shot. She had a lot of questions to answer. "I'm certain."

She stepped back, letting her hands fall to her side. "How did it happen?"

"Let's get out of here."

She nodded and walked with him toward his car, waiting impatiently when he stopped to have a word with Lily, who before she left warned him to be careful. Made him wonder what his expression had given away.

Neither he nor Terry spoke again until they were seated across from each other in a corner booth of the crowded coffee shop. Mitch had been too busy trying to gather his wits. Sympathy was okay, but the other emotions that clawed at his resolve worried him.

He took a deep breath. Anything he felt for her was strictly physical, he reminded himself. Nothing that would get him into too much trouble.

"This detective..." Terry inclined her head toward the window even though Lily was long gone. "You trust her?"

He waited for the waitress to pour their coffee and leave. "I'll ask the questions."

She held his gaze. "You must understand that it was dangerous for me to be identified, and possibly still is, therefore..." She frowned, the delicate curve of her left eyebrow lifting in a perfect arch. "How much do you know?"

"You tell me." He stared back, remembering the daughter she'd abandoned. Their daughter. He suddenly didn't give a damn about the worry lines bracketing her mouth. "Then I'll tell you if you're lying. Again."

"I never lied to you." She didn't even blink. "What we spoke of—" She faltered, nearly flinching before she lifted her chin. "That night we...met."

"You mean the night we made love?"

She visibly swallowed, but her gaze still didn't waver.

He resented her new composure. And the way the perfect bow shape of her lips made his body tighten. "Scratch that. We only had sex."

"You are angry, I know." She started to reach out to him, but pulled back her hand when he eyed it with obvious disgust. "Please let me explain."

"You're damn right you'll explain."

Several people turned from their newspapers and blue plate specials to stare, and he cursed himself for having raised his voice. If the academy had taught him anything, it was to control his emotions. But just looking at her sent every instinct, his very equilibrium out of whack. Damn her.

Palms down, she spread her hands on the table as if trying to steady herself. Gone were the long red fingernails that had sensually scraped his back and filled his head with wicked thoughts. Now her nails were short, squared off and unpolished.

He looked up just as she moistened her lips. He resented the way she did that, too. "I'm waiting."

She nodded. "I will, I promise, but please, tell me about Katherine."

He lifted a brow in challenge. "Her name is Hope."

Apprehension darkened her face. She opened her mouth to speak, closed it again and cleared her throat. "Is she sleeping through the night?"

"Yeah."

The fear in her eyes started to ebb. "Surely she's crawling by now."

"Yeah."

Impatience flashed. "You won't make this easy, will you?"

"Nope."

"Then why did you bother to even look for me?"

He leaned forward to bring his gaze level with hers. "So that I know what to tell my daughter when she's old enough to ask why her mother abandoned her."

Terry gasped and drew back as if he'd struck her. "I didn't abandon her. I left her with you because you're her father."

"What the hell does that matter? Lady, you don't know anything about me." He'd snared the attention of fellow diners again, but he was too angry to care.

"You're wrong." Her voice was low, her gaze steady as she ignored the stares. "I know you're a good man."

"Just by sleeping with me?" He quieted his voice this time, but by the way she flinched, it was obvious his words had cut her like a knife.

Her composure was beginning to slip. Storm clouds gathered in her face. "You've made an accusation. Do I not have the right to defend myself?"

He gave a look of indifference and gestured with a wave of his hand for her to continue.

She moistened her lips again. "We talked that night. Really talked. I don't care how angry you are, Mitch, you can't have forgotten how it was. How we…bonded."

"Is that how you remember it?" His flip tone was met with an unrelenting stare that made him uncomfortable. The hurt in her eyes pierced his anger. "Okay, so we talked, we seemed to have a lot in common. That was enough to leave Hope on my doorstep? Oh, excuse me, the wrong doorstep."

"No, of course not." She slumped a little. "I had you investigated." Her head came up, her eyes widening with panic and disbelief as comprehension sunk in. "The wrong doorstep? But—but—" She shook her head, clearly confused. "I thought I was being followed. I didn't want anyone to see where I'd left her. I must have panicked. Oh, God—"

"Forget it. Everything turned out okay. But what's this about having me investigated?"

It took a while for her to return to the present, but when she did, defiance gleamed in her eyes. "Wouldn't you have done the same in my place?"

"Yeah, but—" anger churned in his belly "—I wouldn't have been in your position."

"I'm not an embezzler or a smuggler. I was framed." A slow fury mounted in her face. "Or are you too pious and self-righteous to admit that life isn't black and white? That sometimes innocent people are accused of crimes they didn't commit." She shook her head with disgust. "Maybe I was wrong about you after all."

He stared at her a long time without speaking. Maybe he wasn't being fair. "Okay, give it your best shot."

"All I have is the truth." She lifted her chin. "I know this situation must be difficult for you, considering your own circumstances."

He frowned in confusion.

"Growing up without a father."

His jaw slackened. What the hell was she doing, using what he'd told her as a weapon? "Damn it. This is not about me."

She reached for his hand. He jerked away but she caught it anyway. "Please, Mitch, I didn't mean any harm. I'm just trying to explain. Can't we be civil?"

It was his own damn fault. The night they'd spent together, he'd shared too many personal things...fears and dreams he'd never told another living soul. He cursed at himself, took a deep steadying breath, and tried not to think about how warm and soft her palm felt, pressed to his wrist.

The sound of rush hour traffic burst through the open diner door, and just like every other time someone came or left, Terry's nervous gaze shot in that direction. Tension radiated from her hand and he had the sudden, foolish urge to turn his palm over, intertwine their fingers and give her a reassuring squeeze.

"I'm sorry," he finally murmured, withdrawing his hand. "Truce."

She sighed, making her mouth relax, her expression less grim. "I'll start from the beginning. You probably know most of it, but—" she spread her hands "—I'd like you to hear my version."

He nodded, instructed himself to keep his mouth shut and settled back to listen.

"A couple of months after we met at Mardi Gras, everything hit the fan, as you Americans say." A sad smile curved her lips. "I received a warning that I was about to be arrested for embezzlement and smuggling." She lifted her slim shoulders. "It happened so fast, and the evidence was so damaging, it was difficult for even *me* to believe I wasn't guilty.

"About that same time, I realized I was pregnant. I knew then I couldn't stay and fight. If it meant my name or my baby, there was no choice."

Mitch tried to keep quiet, but not to question her went against his grain. "According to my sources, your family and company are well-respected in Rio.

All That Glitters provides a lot of jobs. Surely you had some other recourse.''

''Your sources must have also informed you of my, uh, colorful reputation.''

The self-reproach in her eyes got to him. ''We'd already talked about that, remember?''

She gave him a small grateful smile. ''I'm sure the reports you received spiced up the facts, yes?''

''Actually, you were much harder on yourself.'' She'd been a party girl, he knew, keeping late nights, leading the social circuit, dating the city's most eligible bachelors. However, after their night of trading confidences, it didn't take much to figure why she'd flaunted herself, heedless of her family's name and position. A father's disapproval, no matter how misplaced, could often have staggering and negative influences.

Or so Mitch understood.

''You are being kind.'' She settled back, looking more relaxed. ''True, my family name is not without power in Rio, but two years ago a certain high-ranking police official took great exception when I informed him I would no longer be seeing him socially.''

''And he would hamper the investigation because of that?''

She laughed softly. ''Again, you are being kind. *Hamper* is a delicate word. Far too delicate for Manuel's monumental ego. And then if he were to find out I was pregnant, too—'' she sent a gaze heavenward, her beautiful almond-shaped eyes making

Mitch's breath catch "—his ego would never recover."

Mitch frowned. "I don't follow."

The amusement was back in her eyes. "Contrary to popular belief, I did not sleep with every man in Rio."

"You rebuffed him," he said, nodding, "and you thought he might be looking for a little payback."

"There was no doubt. Not with Manny." She gave that small, casual shrug of hers, a gesture Mitch associated with many Latin people.

Except with her it looked seductive, feminine. Memories of that night became so vivid he stiffened. She'd captivated him with her exotic eyes and lilting accent, and he'd foolishly expected her to be more sexually experienced. He certainly hadn't been her first lover, but he could tell she hadn't slept around a lot either.

"Anyway," she continued, "I decided my best course of action was to get out of the country. When I realized that someone was after me—Leo Hayes— I was terrified for the safety of my unborn child. I faked my death to get him off my trail. I'm sure you know about that."

He nodded. "The boating accident off Galveston. It was Lily, the investigator I hired, who arranged for a bounty hunter in Rio to look for you. He was the one who found out you'd faked your death."

"Rick Singleton?" A wry smiled twisted her lips. "I don't know if I should thank you or shake you. I've heard he and my sister have, shall we say, gotten very close."

Mitch recalled her talking about Nina. The sisters were polar opposites, but close. "What about your sister? Couldn't she help?"

"She did, but I didn't want to involve Nina too much. She had her hands full running the company." Terry lowered her gaze to stare at her fingernails. "I didn't even tell her I was pregnant."

Again sympathy worked its way into his heart. The last year hadn't been easy for Terry, being on the run, alone and pregnant, then with a baby. Still, he couldn't afford to go soft now. "So why did you come to San Antonio?"

She looked up, and without a trace of apology said, "To investigate you."

"You found caring for a baby wasn't easy, huh?"

At his patronizing tone, anger sparkled in her eyes. "What I found was that it was my duty to protect her, no matter what. While I was working in a hotel in Austin, a dignitary from the Middle East was staying in the suite I had just cleaned. An Associated Press photographer snapped his picture with me in the background. The diplomat's visit was supposed to be a secret so the photo made it to a lot of front pages. Obviously someone could recognize me and know I was still alive. I had to leave immediately."

"So you came here to investigate me?"

"Yes." The lift of her chin was proud and regal, reminding him that a woman with Terry's means was not used to working as a chambermaid. "You *are* Katherine's father."

"Why were you working as a maid? I heard you emptied your personal safe when you left."

She sighed. "Money doesn't go far when you have to pay for silence, arrange a fake death." She smiled a little at that. "And have a baby. I didn't know what else to do. I went to work at All That Glitters right out of university so that was the sum of my experience. But I'd had many maids. I figured, how hard could it be?" She rolled her gaze heavenward. "Now I know."

Mitch picked up his mug and smiled. He had to give her some credit. "When did you get to San Antonio?"

She smiled back, briefly. "Three days before I left Katherine with you. We were almost the victims of a hit-and-run. I couldn't be sure if it was coincidental or not."

The sip of coffee he'd just taken slid like acid down his throat. "You were almost run down?"

She nodded slowly, her expression blank. "I was holding Katherine and crossing the street in a well-marked crosswalk. The car came out of nowhere, and when I tried to run to the sidewalk, we both fell to the ground. Luckily, we weren't hurt, but I couldn't take the chance it was an accident."

"So you brought her to me," Mitch said, half to himself as he digested the new information. Had he misjudged Terry?

"I didn't see that I had much choice. But at least at that point I'd found out enough about you that I felt comfortable leaving her in your care."

He sat in silence, trying to understand the dangerous new emotion churning in his belly. She hadn't unloaded the baby just because things got rough.

She'd sought protection for their daughter. Just as he would have done.

Still, there were the embezzlement and smuggling charges. She hadn't been cleared of them. Maybe she never would....

"Mitch?"

He blinked, and her face came into focus. Fear drew her dark brows together as she waited for him to snap out of his musings.

"I'm listening," he said absently, and took another sip of coffee while he cleared his head.

"I never intended to keep Katherine's birth from you...it was a matter of timing because of my trouble in Rio. And I had to be sure you were—" she shrugged helplessly "—that you were the man I thought you were."

"Apparently I passed the test." His tone was more flip than he'd intended, although he wasn't sure how he felt about being evaluated as father material before his rights were granted.

Temper flashed like emerald shards in her eyes. "You would have done differently?"

"I don't know. I've never been accused of smuggling."

"How very fortunate for you." She didn't blink, just kept her gaze steady, her hands calmly folded on the table, but he could tell he'd hurt her.

The eyes, she'd told him that night, told you everything about a person. Right now, hers were so bleak he felt like the biggest jerk this side of the Rio Grande.

"Look, Terry, I'm sorry." He scrubbed at his face

and sighed. His jaw felt rough. Had he even bothered to shave today? "I only found out where you were a couple of hours ago. Obviously I didn't give myself time to prepare for..." He exhaled. What did he want to say? Prepare himself against the physical hold she seemed to have over him?

He shook his head. "I thought I knew what I wanted to say to you. Obviously there is more to the story than I anticipated."

"Don't apologize. I know it's hard to suddenly be a single parent." She smiled wryly. "I remember you telling me that you have no siblings and that your mother passed away. But I also knew you were on leave from the FBI and could probably manage with Katherine until you hired some help.

"Oh, and I'm sorry about your injury. It was your Achilles tendon, yes?" He nodded, trying not to make too much of the genuine concern in her eyes. "You seem better now. Have you decided if you want to return to your post?"

He started to voice the doubts about his career that had circled inside his head for the past few months, to explain his decision to accept a position as a deputy sheriff. He stopped himself, amazed that it was still so easy to talk to Terry. That he actually wanted to unload his fears on her. "Let's not get sidetracked. You still have questions to answer."

"Of course." At his abrupt tone, her smile faded. "Let me tell you what else I know about you."

"That's not necessary. Where we go from here is what we need to—"

She cut him off. "I also found out that you are

financially secure due to sound investing, and that you send a generous check every other month to the Big Brothers organization.''

Mitch frowned. He'd done a lot of investigative work for the Bureau over the years. Being on the receiving end sucked. ''Okay, so you did your homework—''

''I'm not finished,'' Terry said, cutting him off again. ''Three years ago you intercepted a bullet to save your partner, and you've been decorated on two other occasions for bravery. Your friends think there is not a more honorable man on this earth, and they would trust you with the lives of their children. That, Agent Barnes, is what made my decision to entrust you with my daughter.''

He shifted uncomfortably, wondering at the growing anger on her face.

''But frankly, I'm a little concerned,'' she continued. ''The man sitting across from me is not that man.''

''What?''

''You've already judged me, haven't you? I thought you Americans believed in a person being innocent until proven guilty?''

Mitch's blood simmered. ''What do I know about you? Other than what my investigator turned up. I'll tell you. You're a quitter.''

Her eyes widened, and then narrowed in anger. ''How dare you— I explained why I had to leave Katherine with you.''

''Yeah? And why did you leave that night we met?''

She blinked, and her expression grew grim. "I didn't have a choice. My life was complicated enough. There was no future for us."

"So, you made that decision for us both?"

"You don't understand."

"Damn right I don't."

She stiffened, and pushed her untouched coffee aside. "I want to see Katherine."

The pain of Terry's abandonment that morning felt so raw and fresh it amazed Mitch. "Her name is Hope." He paused, until the fear in Terry's eyes got to him. She hadn't had an easy time of it either. "Hayes is dead so there's no threat. No reason why you can't see her."

"I suppose." She looked unsure.

"Something else you want to tell me?"

"No, but what if the hit-and-run wasn't an accident?"

"Then it must've been Hayes, and he's dead now." Suspicion needled him. "Unless you've left something out and someone else is after you."

She shook her head. "Though sometimes I get the feeling someone's watching me."

He stared at her a moment, trying to gauge her sincerity.

"It's probably paranoia after looking over my shoulder for so many months." She frowned suddenly. "Unless the Brazilian officials—"

"No, they would have picked you up, not kept you under surveillance."

"Of course."

"Unless they think you can lead them to something they want?"

She evenly met his gaze. "Like I said, I'm being paranoid. Can we go see...Hope Katherine now?"

After laying some money on the table, he slid out of the booth. "Let's go."

He didn't miss Terry's glance over her shoulder as they stepped out onto the sidewalk.

CHAPTER THREE

TERRY'S QUEASY stomach churned like a cauldron of Baba's magic potions. Her childhood nanny had always had a cure or hex for everything. Terry had ignored the woman's superstitions, but right now, she'd try just about anything to calm her nerves.

Would Katherine recognize her? Would she resent having been deprived of her mother's milk so early? Had she felt abandoned? Did babies recognize that sort of thing? There was still so much Terry had to learn about being a mother.

As for Mitch, she didn't know quite what she'd expected from him. That he took good care of their daughter should have been the only thing she wanted. Certainly not a more enthusiastic reunion with her. But her heavy heart told her otherwise.

"You have a wonderful home, Mitch," she said as he led her through the brightly decorated living room. Oddly, it reminded her of something one would find in Rio.

"Nothing like you're used to, I'm sure."

Annoyed at his snide remark, she pasted a bland smile on her face. "You're right. I have a tiny efficiency downtown."

The way he averted his gaze told her she'd hit her

target. Good. How dare he judge her? She hadn't chosen to be brought up with wealth and luxury. Most people didn't understand how much responsibility accompanied the so-called privilege. Besides, a lot of good the Monteverde name and money did her now.

"Hope's room is this way." He preceded her down a short hall, and then stopped abruptly at an open door and frowned. "She's not here. Neither is her stroller. Margaret must have taken her for a walk."

"The nanny," Terry said absently as she moved closer for a peek inside.

She immediately spotted the porcelain doll she'd left with Katherine and she breathed with relief. There were many other toys surrounding the ornate white crib over which hung a Disney mobile. Too many. It made her smile.

"What a lovely nursery."

"I don't know." An endearing frown drew his dark brows together. "It's awfully pink."

"She's a girl. Pink is good."

"Sounds sexist to me."

Terry laughed. "It's called tradition. We'll all outgrow it before it becomes a problem."

At the resentment that entered his blue eyes, her smile faltered. Not just resentment, but accusation, anger, regret all mixed together. Was it her reference to *we* that had triggered the response? Or was it simply her own insecurity over her rights to Katherine? Fear formed a lump in her throat, and she had to struggle for her next breath.

"There's a park nearby they sometimes go to,"

Mitch said when the silence became uncomfortable. "They shouldn't be long."

"I hope not." A shiver ran down her spine and she rubbed her arms. "It'll be dark soon."

"Don't worry. Margaret's reliable." This time compassion flickered in his eyes, reminding Terry of the kind man she remembered. "Margaret's been a big help to me. I was lucky to find her. Let's go to the kitchen and have something to drink."

Terry's misgivings eased. She'd lived with paranoia for so long it was difficult not to see a threat at every turn. Katherine was safe, that was the important thing. Mitch had taken good care of their daughter, just like she knew he would.

She followed him, admiring the snug fit of his jeans, how his broad shoulders seemed to fill the space between the cream-colored walls. Firsthand knowledge that he was firm and muscled under those clothes made her body grow warm, her nerves jump again.

"Perhaps you have a little wine in your kitchen?" she asked, belatedly wondering how wise drinking alcohol would be.

He shot her a questioning look over his shoulder. "There's both Chardonnay and beer in the fridge. I'll get the glasses."

They entered the modest-size kitchen, made airy and bright with yellow sunflower wallpaper and a spotless white tile floor.

The white marbled counters were clean and free of clutter except for an old toaster and state-of-the-art blender.

He opened an upper cabinet near the sink, while she headed for the refrigerator. It was brand-new and large enough for a family of five. She opened it and stared at the crowded top two shelves.

More than a dozen containers were stacked on top of each other, each one labeled and dated—carrots, peas, applesauce, spinach…. Terry took out one of the small square containers and peered more closely at it.

"Mitch?" Ignoring the bottle of wine tucked back in the corner, she turned to him. "Is this what I think it is?"

He seemed slightly embarrassed, and shrugged. "Hope likes homemade baby food better than the store-bought stuff."

Terry smiled. "Ah, did she tell you that?"

He gave her a gruff look.

She returned the container and reached for the wine. "How far in advance does Margaret make these?"

He didn't answer, but made a lot of noise digging in an utensil drawer until he pulled out a corkscrew.

"I'm not being critical. I'm only asking because there are a lot of containers in here and since there aren't any preservatives—"

"Margaret doesn't make them. I do. That batch was made this morning."

"*You?*"

"Yeah, you got a problem with that?"

His defensiveness startled a laugh out of her. "No, I think it's wonderful you're that concerned. I don't understand why you seem uncomfortable admitting it.''

One side of his mouth lifted and he seemed to relax. ''I've got a tough guy image to protect.''

''I see. Tell you what, I promise not to tell anyone you're playing Martha Stewart.''

''Very funny.''

She laughed at his wry expression. ''Want me to get you a beer?''

She remembered that was his preference, and wondered at the wariness in his gaze as he nodded.

She got out one of the three remaining bottles of Heineken, and then watched as he opened the Chardonnay. A warm feeling blossomed in her chest as she noticed the way his biceps bunched as he worked to free the cork.

He had to be about thirty-seven by now, but he had the body of a younger man. From working out, she knew, keeping fit in order to be the best he could at his job. Even now, after being sidelined for several months, he still had not a spare ounce of flesh on him.

Terry turned away to find some napkins. He had a great body, no question about it. But that wasn't what had drawn her to him. There was so much more to the man, like his sense of honor and duty, his tolerant acceptance. She smiled to herself. He was the kind of man who made his daughter special baby food.

''Are you hungry? I think we have leftover meat loaf.''

She shook her head. ''My stomach's a little jumpy.''

His gaze narrowed. "Hope is fine. She's been well cared for. I promise you that."

"Oh, no, I'm not worried about her. She couldn't have been in better hands." She sighed. "But it's been so long since I've seen her and—and I'm just being silly."

He set the corkscrew aside, his expression softening. "Think she won't remember you?"

Terry gave a half shrug.

Mitch smiled. "I bet as soon as she hears your voice, she'll give you a big dimpled grin."

"She has dimples?"

"One." He slowly closed the distance between them. "Right here," he said, touching the middle of Terry's cheek.

She held her breath, and stared up into his vivid blue eyes, waiting for him to dip his head, bring his lips to hers. Instead, he reached around her and grabbed the beer she'd set on the counter, then moved away.

Foolish disappointment nudged her, and she quickly stepped aside. She grabbed the wineglass he'd set on the counter and filled it with a tad too much Chardonnay.

Who had she been trying to fool? She knew damn well what she wanted from Mitch. Him. She wanted him to feel the same way about her as she did about him. The sex had been great the night they met, but it had meant so much more to her than just a physical act.

He'd touched her soul that night, taught her about acceptance—of herself, her father. Not a day went by that she hadn't thought about Mitch. At times she'd even convinced herself there was a way for them to be together—that maybe the possibility wasn't so hopeless.

She'd left him that night, knowing there was no room left in her life for regret and disappointment. Obligation and duty to her family and All That Glitters motivated all her decisions. Her time was not her own, and her father would never have approved. Mitch was an outsider, a world apart from their social and cultural circle.

And then the accusations had started, the charges brought against her so fast she hadn't been able to totally comprehend the depth of her trouble. When she'd discovered she was pregnant, all her energy turned toward survival.

Still, in the middle of the night, when she tossed and turned, wondering how Katherine was faring with her father, Terry had harbored the hope they could be a family once her legal trouble was over.

Clearly it had been a foolish dream. She still thought Mitch was a good man, and she didn't blame him for his suspicion or bitterness. All that mattered was that he be a good father to Katherine.

"I have an idea."

She looked over to find Mitch staring thoughtfully at her. "What's that?"

"How long has it been since you spoke with your sister?"

"Nina?" Terry inhaled deeply, the slight odor of a lemon-scented cleaner making her queasy. "A while." Terry knew Nina had returned to Rio, but she hadn't risked calling. "It isn't safe to have contact."

"Not anymore." He pulled his cell phone out of his pocket and handed it to her.

She accepted the small instrument but shook her head. It was too risky to call. Nevertheless, she glanced at the clock and calculated the time difference between San Antonio and Rio. Knowing Nina, she would still be at the office. "Hayes may be dead, but the police are still looking for me. Surely they have All That Glitters' phones tapped."

"Probably. But if you use that phone, you won't have to worry about it."

Wistful excitement stirred in her belly. It had been so long since she'd heard her sister's voice. "What do you mean?"

"It's my company issue phone." His gaze held hers steady, telling her more than his words. "Calls from it can't be traced."

"But..." She moistened her lips. Of course he knew what he was talking about, and she believed him... "Will you get in trouble?"

His lips curved in a slow, lazy smile. "Let me worry about that."

"Mitch..."

He moved closer, until he was a breath away, and put a silencing finger to her lips. "Call her, Terry. Don't argue. Just call."

She swallowed, nodded.

He didn't retreat. Instead his gaze lingered where his finger brushed across her lower lip. The hunger in his eyes made her pulse quicken, her knees weak. If he kissed her, she didn't know what would happen. It didn't matter. She wanted him, and it was gratifying to know he still wanted her.

"I'll be in the living room," he said, dropping his hand with an abruptness that jolted her. "So you can make your call in private."

She muttered something, and hoped it resembled a thank-you.

Not that he stayed long enough to hear it. He'd disappeared as quickly as a magician's rabbit.

He was being prudent, she told herself as she punched in the numbers to All That Glitters. Halfway through the process she jabbed the wrong number and had to start over. This wasn't the time or place to renew their physical attraction. Perhaps there never would be a time. The thought saddened her.

A voice Terry didn't recognize answered her sister's private line, and she almost hung up. Instead she took a quick breath and asked for Nina. The second she heard her sister's familiar voice, tears sprang to Terry's eyes. She blinked them away.

"Nina?"

"Yes—Terry?" Nina's normally reserved pitch rose with excitement. "Terry!"

"It's me."

"Where are you—no, do not tell me. Are you all right? Is anything wrong?"

Terry laughed softly. "I'm fine. Slow down."

"Thank God. I have so much news for you. Can you talk?"

"For a short time."

"Leo Hayes is dead."

"I heard."

"You did? But you are not in Rio—never mind. Do not tell me."

Nostalgia warmed Terry as she pictured her sister's fretful and impatient frown. "I'm not in Rio, and I know nothing other than that he is dead."

"Oh, but there is so much more, Teresa. Not only is he no longer a threat to you, but the police may have found enough evidence in his hotel room to clear you of the smuggling charge and…"

"Calm down, Nina." Terry's head was spinning. Overly excited, her sister alternated between English and Portuguese, and Terry was too addled herself to make sense of it all. "Did Manuel tell you they would drop the charges?"

"Not exactly. Rick—he is a bounty hunter—do you know about him?"

"I learned that the two of you have become quite close."

Nina laughed. "There is so much to tell you. Rick is actually the one who came up with the leads and pointed out inconsistencies in the case. Manuel is still being stubborn, but he will not be able to ignore the evidence for long."

Terry briefly closed her eyes and tried not to get too excited. She was still a long way from being cleared.

"There is something else." Nina paused. "This news is not so good. Apparently, there is someone in the company who had been helping Hayes."

"Who?" She shook her head with denial. "I can't

believe that. Everyone who works for us has been there for years. We know them all personally.''

''We do not know who, but the evidence indicates that—''

''The evidence once indicated *I* was guilty.''

''True, but it is unrealistic to think Hayes was able to transport his diamonds out of the country hidden in our shipments without inside help.''

Terry sighed. Her sister was right, but to seek out someone else, someone they knew and trusted, in order for Terry to escape suspicion seemed so wrong.

''Terry?'' Nina said after a brief, uncomfortable silence. ''I know what you are thinking, but if one of our employees is doing something illegal, we need to find out.''

''Of course. It makes sense that someone internally would be involved with the embezzlement setup as well.'' It was just so damn hard to believe that a person she knew and trusted could hate her that much they'd set up a phony Swiss bank account to incriminate her.

Nina made a soft sound of exasperation Terry recognized well. It meant more bad news. ''You might as well know, Meg Turner is being investigated.''

''No, not Meg.'' Quiet, studious, unassuming, the woman had been a straight-A student the entire four years Terry had known her at Northwestern University. Though they'd never actually been close friends, Terry knew her well enough. ''Whoever came up with that theory couldn't be more wrong.''

''I knew you'd feel this way, and I wish I could

agree with you, but the situation doesn't look good for her.''

Several months after graduation, Meg had gone to Rio, and Terry had hired her on the spot. For nearly ten years she had been a loyal and reliable employee. ''What does she say about the charges?''

''No one knows. She disappeared about a month ago.''

Oxygen deserted her lungs, and her head grew light. ''Disappeared? Without quitting or saying anything to anyone?''

''Oh, she turned in a letter of resignation. It was left on my desk one evening, and then no one saw her again. Rick checked her apartment. It was cleaned out.''

Terry sank onto a kitchen chair, trying to make sense of the impossible. ''Meg had always been happy working for us. She said it was her dream to come to Rio.''

''I know,'' Nina said quietly. ''I am sorry.''

''There still may be a reasonable explanation.''

''Of course that is possible.''

Terry closed her eyes and tried to picture her oceanfront apartment, her corner office overlooking the city. Stress and time had made her memory fuzzy. It seemed like decades since she'd been home.

Even Nina sounded like she'd changed. Of course she'd had to. The responsibility of running All That Glitters had fallen on her shoulders.

''Terry, are you still there?''

She opened her eyes. Reality awaited. ''I was just thinking about how much you've changed.''

"I was thinking the same thing about you earlier."

A wry smile lifted the corners of her mouth. It was true. They had both changed. Shy, reserved Nina had blossomed and taken charge of both her life and the company. Terry, who had always been the more gregarious and flamboyant one, had learned humility, and a true sense of responsibility.

Of course she'd always taken her leadership role seriously, especially after her invalid father had been forced to step down, but she hadn't known deep abiding commitment until she'd had Katherine. Motherhood had changed many of her attitudes and goals.

"Yes, Nina, we have both changed. For the better, yes?"

"I must admit, for me, it has been good that the demands of the business have forced me out of my shell. But I worry about you. Do you have any happiness in your life anymore?"

Terry winced at the concern in her little sister's voice. Except Nina wasn't so little anymore. "You needn't worry about me. Even though I couldn't be with her these past few months, Katherine has brought me so much joy. Someday when you have a child you'll understand."

Nina sighed, and then with enough hesitancy to make Terry's skin prickle with dread, said, "That is something else about me that has changed."

"What?"

"Now, do not get upset."

"Nina! Tell me." A scary thought occurred to Terry. "You're pregnant?"

"No. Not yet anyway. But I am a married woman.

Father Pereira married Rick and me last week." She paused. "I'm sorry, Teresa, I wanted to wait until you were here but I did not know when you would come back. I really hated to—"

"Shh, Nina, I'm not upset. I'm thrilled for you," she whispered, letting the news sink in. Even though she'd suspected what was coming, it was still hard to believe her little sister was married. "Truly, I am. Too bad Mama wasn't here to fuss over you. She would have given you a grand reception. One better even than Mardis Gras."

"I don't want a party. I want you here."

"I want that, too. And I want you to meet your niece."

"I can hardly wait. You will like Rick. He is very good to me, and he is working hard to clear your name."

"Look, we've been talking a long time. Perhaps—" She stopped herself before she said Mitch's name. If the lines were still tapped, no point in giving the police too much information. "Perhaps I will be able to call again soon."

"One more thing before we hang up."

Terry was suddenly anxious to end the call. A horrible, wistful envy had slithered its way into her psyche. She hated that she could be envious of her own sister, whom she loved indescribably. But the panicky feeling threatening her composure filled her with such a desperate sense of loss she couldn't think straight.

Of course she hadn't lost Nina simply because she'd gotten married, and intellectually Terry knew that. But fear festered and clawed at her, made her glance nervously out the kitchen window. Had she lost Katherine, too?

She took two deep breaths and ordered herself to calm down. This was exhaustion and panic talking. Soon this entire mess would be cleaned up and she'd be back in Rio, sitting in her office, behind her desk, immersed once again in her old life, too busy to worry about the past. Except she'd have Katherine to go home to at night.

Assuming Mitch didn't interfere....

Oh, God, she couldn't bear the thought of losing her daughter.

"Terry, have you listened to anything I have said?"

"I'm sorry, Nina. The connection is starting to break up."

"I know this is an awful time to discuss something so important, but I do not know when we will speak again. But I am only asking you to think about it."

"Think about what?"

"Selling All That Glitters."

CHAPTER FOUR

LONG AFTER Terry disconnected the call, she sat at the kitchen table and stared out the window. Running All That Glitters was all she knew how to do. Except for the years she'd studied at Northwestern in Chicago, she'd worked at the company in some capacity since she was fourteen. And even while at the university, she'd gone home and worked during the summers.

But then there was Nina, who never wanted to be involved in the running of the business at all, and God only knew when Terry would be able to return. It certainly wasn't fair to insist her sister continue to carry the burden of president and CEO, when designing jewelry was her real passion. Terry shook her head, her heart so heavy she had no desire to raise herself from the chair.

"You finished your call?"

She looked up at the sound of Mitch's voice, and met his concerned eyes. "Yes, I just hung up. I'm sorry it was such a lengthy call. It had been a long time since we talked."

"Don't worry about it." He looked uncertain for a moment, and then asked, "Is anything wrong back home?"

She shook her head and stood. "Actually, it looks as though I may soon be cleared of the smuggling charge."

"That's terrific news."

"They found evidence in Leo Hayes's hotel room that may help prove my innocence."

He frowned. "I'd think you'd look a little happier about it."

She wasn't about to discuss her personal feelings with him. "Aren't they back yet?"

His gaze was long and probing. "No, let's go into the living room. We'll be able to see them come down the drive."

Nodding, she grabbed the half-full glass of wine.

He stepped aside to let her pass, then reached out when she got closer, and laid a gentle hand on her arm. "I'm a good listener if you need one."

She hesitated, and then slowly met his gaze. "I know."

He smiled, and she sagged against him.

"Hey, what's the matter?" He put both arms around her and drew her closer still. "Sounds like things are looking up."

"They are," she muttered. "I'm just being silly."

When she tried to pull away, he held on and nudged her chin up. "I doubt you've been silly a day in your life. What's wrong?"

The sincerity in his eyes was nearly her undoing. She shrugged helplessly. "I miss Nina. I miss Katherine. I miss my life." She sniffed. "Well, not all of it."

"Ah, Terry." He tucked her head under his chin and hugged her tighter. "It's been hell, hasn't it?"

"I'm not looking for sympathy." She stiffened and tried to retreat again.

He held firm. "Tough. You deserve some."

Her heart pounded so hard, surely he felt it slamming against his chest. "Mitch?" She tilted her head back to look at him.

As soon as she saw the desire and compassion in his eyes, she forgot everything else. Her lips parted, but nothing came out. She should move away from him. She couldn't do that either.

He lowered his head and she offered her mouth. He didn't hesitate to capture it, keeping the kiss gentle at first, nibbling, brushing. But when she shifted and her breasts pressed against his chest, a low groan vibrated in his throat and he thrust his tongue into her mouth.

She got rid of the wine, slid her palms up his chest and gripped his shoulders, raising herself on tiptoes to give him better access. Her eagerness fueled his hunger and he reached down to cup her buttocks, hauling her tighter against him. He was hard and ready and it startled her how mindlessly easy it was to crave the feel of his naked body again. To want to escape her problems by soaking up the comfort he offered.

Allowing herself a small taste of heaven, she kissed him back, hard, thoroughly, letting his hands explore her backside, using her mouth to feed their fever. Mitch shifted, and she realized they were both moving, slowly, her backward, until her fanny hit the kitchen counter.

She gasped when he gripped her around the waist and lifted her onto the cool marble countertop. He immediately parted her legs and slipped between them to stand in front of her while he undid her top button.

"We shouldn't do this," she whispered.

"I know." He slid the second button out of the hole.

"Katherine and the nanny could be home at any moment."

"We'll hear Margaret unlock the front door." With a jerk of impatience, he pulled the last two buttons free.

"Mitch?"

He wouldn't look up. He stared at the skin above her black lace bra, tracing the dip of her cleavage with his gaze, until his restless hands moved up to cup her breasts.

Her breath caught when he unhooked the front clasp and pushed the lace aside. Her breasts sprang free, her nipples already hard and ripe, and she thought she'd die waiting for him to cover them with his mouth. His hand was a little unsteady as he slipped it under her breast and palmed the weight, his mouth lowering to hers.

He touched his tongue to the tip of her pearled nipple, and then hooked his free arm around her waist when she jumped, pulling her closer to his greedy mouth. Her entire nipple disappeared between his lips as he suckled like a starving man.

"Oh, Mitch, please—"

He abandoned her left breast but immediately nipped at her right one, nibbling, sucking, his eagerness making her moist and ready.

Her breath came in small embarrassing pants as she cupped his shoulders for support and dug her fingers into his straining muscles. She thought he would stop when he abruptly pulled away, but he covered her mouth with his again and plunged inside.

Sweet, hot desire saturated her senses and nearly banished her misgivings. This was Mitch, the man she'd dreamed about for over a year. How could this be wrong?

It wouldn't. Not at any other time. But right now, there were too many issues to settle, like custody of their child, and her own unquestionable innocence. Sex was an added complication neither of them needed.

She drew back. "Mitch, we can't."

He followed her, leaning forward, trying to maintain contact, his breath warm and seductive against her lips.

Summoning all her willpower, she lowered her hands and flattened her palms firmly against his chest. He immediately stopped his pursuit. She almost hauled him back.

"I've missed you, Terry." His voice was low, nearly inaudible. "So damn much."

A foolish longing tightened her belly. He missed the sex. That's what he meant, and she'd do well not to misunderstand. "We did some pretty amazing things together, didn't we?"

Confusion flitted across his face, and then the warmth in his eyes turned to ice. He stepped back, his gaze falling to her breasts, lingering for a moment before he met her eyes. The sudden shift in his mood had her pulling the front of her shirt together.

"Yeah, we did," he said, the indifference in his tone filling her with regret.

Perhaps she'd sounded too flip. She'd only wanted to reassure him that she understood the superficial nature of their relationship, and that he had nothing to fear from her. Was it possible he wanted more, as well? Her pulse quickened at the thought, and her hand reflexively went out to him.

He eyed it briefly before turning away. "I'll meet you in the living room."

She should let him go. Pretend nothing happened. "Mitch?"

He stopped, but his reluctance couldn't be more obvious in the way his body tensed and he refused to look at her.

Terry swallowed, her courage slipping. "I'll only be a minute."

He nodded, and left without a word or glance.

What the hell had happened? One minute he was undressing her, and the next he seemed barely able to remain in the same room? With her shaky hands, it took twice as long to button her blouse as it should have.

She slid off the counter and grabbed her wineglass. There was only one sip left, which she gratefully swallowed, and then thought about having another before facing him again. Instead, she set the glass aside, smoothed her hair and lifted her chin.

Mitch stared out the front window, trying to cool off. Both physically and mentally. Bad enough he'd let his groin do the thinking, but now, even as he realized how foolish he'd been to start in with Terry, his body still wouldn't calm down. He'd have to change his jeans if things didn't settle down soon.

Although he'd purposely kept his gaze out the window, he knew the second she entered the room. It was as if she was north and his body was a compass. It pointed right at her. He shifted, hoping to ease the strain at his fly.

Her scent was probably what alerted him. Feminine, mysterious, seductive, it scrambled his senses, impaired his judgment. He'd best remember its power. Especially since his body seemed to have a mind of its own where she was concerned.

Out of the corner of his eye, he saw her settle at the end of the couch, curling her legs beneath her firm round bottom. She had the most incredible body, soft, yet hard and curved in all the right places—the kind that ended up between the pages of magazines. Except Terry had too much class and grace to allow herself to be exploited that way.

But would she use her charms to disarm him? When it came to the welfare of their daughter, there wasn't much he wouldn't do himself.

"I'm a little worried." Her voice was soft, tentative. "Shouldn't they be back by now?"

"Not necessarily."

"But if they went to the park, they usually don't stay more than a couple of hours."

He swung a look at her. "How do you know?"

Her eyes widened slightly. "I don't." She shrugged. "I'm just guessing."

It was clear she was lying by the way she picked at a loose thread on her sleeve when he tried to hold her gaze. He let silence lapse, waiting for her to explain.

"Okay, so I've spied on my own daughter. Is that a crime?"

He slowly shook his head, her admission both surprising and pleasing him.

"I know it was risky." She crossed her arms and rubbed them. "But I was extremely careful and I never got close. I kept so much distance I could barely see the color of her outfits."

"I'm surprised you even stuck around San Antonio."

Pain and guilt darkened her eyes and she slowly shook her head. "I know I should have gotten as far away from Katherine as possible. But I couldn't bring myself to—" She sighed. "Anyway, I knew she'd be safe with you."

He glanced at his watch. Not to check the time but because it hurt him to see the anguish in her face. She'd been forced to separate from her child and the decision had cost her. He couldn't deny that now. No matter how many defensive walls he wanted to erect.

Still staring at his watch, it dawned on him that Margaret and Hope had been gone a long time. Too long. It wasn't like Margaret to go out near the dinner hour.

"Mitch?"

He looked up.

She gave him a wan smile. "Have I thanked you for taking such good care of my baby?"

Anger, dread, panic all converged at her possessive tone. *Her* baby? Did she think she could waltz back into his and Hope's life and reclaim all rights, just like that? "What else would I do with my own child? Abandon her?"

Terry flinched as if he'd physically dealt a blow. "That's not fair."

"Yeah? And you thought that I'd be ready to hand Hope over just because you have your problems sorted out. Is that fair?"

"I never made that assumption."

He stared at her in long deliberate silence. "I've bonded with her, Terry. She's my daughter in every sense of the word. What did you think would happen?"

Her lips parted as though she wanted to speak, but fear narrowed her eyes and she shrank back, rubbing her arms. She looked small and helpless, and he felt like a jerk.

"The truth?" she finally asked. "I didn't think about anything beyond keeping Katherine safe."

That finished him off. He really was a first class jerk. "You came to San Antonio before the hit-and-run. You had me investigated."

She moistened her lips. "I thought perhaps... I wanted to tell you about Ka—Hope Katherine, and I wanted…'' Her voice trailed off, and the fear was back in her eyes. "I wanted to see you again."

Mitch swallowed. That's what he wanted to hear, wasn't it? So why was he fighting it? Why didn't he want to believe her? "Because of our daughter?"

"There's that, of course." She quit rubbing her arms and hugged herself. "But I also wanted to see if the magic between us was still there."

Magic. That just about described the night they met. But was she referring to the physical or emotional chemistry? "Tell me something. If you hadn't gotten pregnant, or had to leave Rio because of the criminal charges, would you have come looking for me?"

Her brows drew together in a thoughtful frown as she studied the geometric pattern on the armchair. He had to give her credit for not jumping at an easy answer, one that she thought he wanted to hear.

After a long moment, she said, "Yes."

He waited for something more. It didn't come. "Why?"

She sighed. "I'd never met anyone like you."

He shook away the hope building in his gut. "Of course your answer is still hypothetical since—"

"If you want to keep me at arm's length, then just be honest."

He exhaled sharply at her blunt offensive. "I'm merely being practical."

"Really?"

The amusement in her eyes and voice annoyed the hell out of him. "You suddenly know me so well?"

"Would you rather think that I'm sacrificing myself for my daughter? So that she can have a father in her life? Would this have anything to do with your father abandoning you?''

"I don't know that." He cursed himself for responding. His personal life, especially his past, was not open for discussion. Thinking about it would only muddy the waters. God knew he had enough unanswered questions of his own. "Don't try to turn the tables. It won't work."

The amusement was gone and her expression softened. "I'm not trying to open old wounds—"

He put a hand up to stop her. The conflicting maneuvers going on in his head the last few months had played hell on his emotions. Although he'd made an effort to find his father, the man who'd abandoned his mother, Mitch knew his attempts had been half-assed at best.

So far all he knew was that the guy could be a salesman from Kansas or a cowboy from San Antonio. Allowing his cynicism to take over, Mitch had let the ball drop and eased up on his search. Neither candidate sounded like the kind of upstanding, long haul, ready-to-take-on-a-family kind of man.

Yet there was still a part of him that wanted to know the man, face him with all the questions that had plagued Mitch over the years. The same part that harbored a youthful hope that he hadn't been abandoned. That there was a reasonable explanation why he'd had to grow up without the guidance of a father.

He focused on Terry. Desperation was a reason.

She stared back at him, the fragile uncertainty in her face making him regret his sharpness.

He raked a hand through his hair. "Look, we're both tense. This is all new and we— Let's shelve the heavy talk for now."

"Fine." She turned abruptly toward the window, tossing back her hair with a haughty flip of her head. "I've grown accustomed to unfounded accusations."

"Terry…"

Her eyes blazed when she looked back at him. "I did not find you only because I was in trouble. You had a right to know about your daughter, and foolish me thought maybe we had something worth exploring. That's it. You can believe what you want."

Mitch took a deep breath. God, he wanted to believe it. But all he had was her say-so. And how much did he really know about Terry? Nothing other than what Lily and the other detectives he'd hired had told him.

And what Terry herself had poured out to him the night they met. They had both pretty thoroughly exposed themselves. Later he'd spent hours wondering what the hell had gotten into him to have allowed his fears and feelings to bleed like a fresh-cut vein. He'd tried to blame it on the wine, the full moon, the excitement of Mardi Gras that scented the balmy Rio air.

But he knew deep down it was the woman who'd silently convinced him to let down his guard, seek her confidence and the comfort she'd freely given.

Her heartfelt sigh brought him out of his preoccupation. She sat with her hands clasped, her fingers tightly interwoven, not nearly as composed as she'd have him think. It wouldn't kill him to give her the benefit of the doubt.

He offered a conciliatory smile. "I've been an ass. Forgive me?"

Suspicion briefly narrowed her gaze. "You need no forgiveness." She relaxed some. "I don't blame you for being cautious. I suppose you have no reason to believe me. I shouldn't take it personally."

He didn't agree, or dispute her. He merely kept silent, figuring he at least owed her the floor.

She stared off out the window. Mitch glanced at his watch again. Now he was getting worried.

"I have something I want to show you." Terry uncurled her legs. "There was a doll I left with Hope Katherine. I saw it briefly when you showed me her room."

He nodded. "It's one of her favorites."

An odd smile curved her mouth. "It was once my mother's and then mine, but it's much more valuable now."

He'd figured it was some sort of antique and only let Hope touch it when she was supervised. Good thing. Obviously the doll meant a lot to Terry.

"May I go get it?"

He smiled. "Of course."

The phone rang as soon as she stood, and he got up to get it. Terry hesitated, concern in her eyes.

As soon as he answered, he knew it was trouble. The voice was garbled, so that it was difficult to identify the gender of the caller. It could be a wrong number, maybe some drunk looking for a ride home, but after years with the Bureau it was hard to ignore the uneasiness rising in his gut. He tried to avoid Terry's eyes. No use worrying her yet.

"Hello?" he said for the second time.

"Look in the dresser," the voice said.

"Who is this?" he asked, and Terry clutched his arm.

"Do it."

"I don't know what you're talking about. Tell me who you are or I'm hanging up."

"Hope's dresser. Top drawer."

Fear exploded like an atomic bomb, ravaging his insides, destroying his ability to breathe. This couldn't be happening. Not to him. He'd worked cases like this. Kidnappings were other people's nightmares.

He forced himself to take a deep breath, trying to chase the panic robbing him of reason. "Okay, I'm headed that way. Don't hang up."

Terry's nails dug into his arm as she followed him. "Who is it? What's happening?"

The caller's evil laugh grated in his ear.

And then there was a click.

"Hello?"

"Mitch." Terry's nails dug deeper. "Please."

He threw the phone across the room. "He said to check the dresser drawer."

"Who?"

Mitch ran to Hope's room with Terry right behind him. He yanked the top drawer so hard it left its tracks and crashed to the floor. He saw the note lying on top of Hope's pink sleeper.

In bold black letters were the words "Don't Call The Cops—Or She Dies."

CHAPTER FIVE

KNEELING BESIDE MITCH, Terry stared at the words, refusing to believe them. Hope Katherine was supposed to be safe here with her father. How could this happen? How could he *let* this happen?

She turned her accusing gaze at him. He was pale, his expression one of total shock. He was hurting, too. She didn't care. "You did this."

Slowly he turned to look at her, his stricken eyes giving her pause. He said nothing, only stared in stunned disbelief.

"You couldn't leave well enough alone. You had to look for me. Now this—" Her voice broke along with her heart and she sank onto her heels.

"Blaming each other won't help us get Hope back." Mitch's gaze was steady, firm, but fear haunted his face. "The kidnapper will call again to make his demand, and we need to remain calm so we know best how to analyze the situation. Statistically, if it's money the kidnapper wants—"

Terry shook her head in astonishment as she forced herself to her feet. "Analyze the situation? This is our daughter we're talking about. How can you stand there and treat this like one of your anonymous cases?"

"Would you prefer I fall apart?"

His quiet words pierced her defenses. She almost sank back to the floor. "You were supposed to keep her safe," she whispered.

"I know."

She took in a big gulp of air, blinked away the panic threatening to well up in her eyes. "I'm sorry."

Mitch grabbed her upper arms with gentle hands and ducked his head to look her in the face. "We'll get her back. Do you understand?"

She gave him a weak nod, and he pulled her against his chest. When he slid his arms around her, she didn't resist. She leaned into his quiet strength, accepting his comfort and praying like she never had before.

It wasn't Mitch's fault. It was hers for not warning him. He had no idea how high the stakes were, or what Leo Hayes was capable of....

Terry stiffened. But Hayes was dead.

She pulled back and looked up at Mitch. "Who would—"

His expression was so grim it sent a shiver down her spine. "I was hoping you might have an idea."

"Oh, God."

"What?"

Shaking her head, she shrugged helplessly. "Unless Hayes had a partner, I don't know anyone...."

His sigh was harsh with disgust. "If he did, that would have come to light by now." He let her go and paced to the window, running a hand through his hair, strain creasing his face. "What about that police official?"

"Manuel? He's spiteful and jealous, but not a criminal."

"You're sure?"

She briefly closed her eyes. She wasn't sure about anything anymore. "He wouldn't steal a child."

"Money can make a person do ugly things." Mitch exhaled loudly. "But he's not a logical candidate. He would've had to familiarize himself with the area, get to know Margaret's routine and mine. He didn't have time to do that without his absence being noticed."

Terry straightened suddenly. "What about Margaret?"

"Margaret?" He frowned, and then swore. "I hadn't even given the poor woman a thought. But it's not likely the kidnapper would have taken her, too. She's probably knocked out cold somewhere." He stared out the window. "She may be able to help us, though."

"No, I meant, what do you know about her?"

He shot her a look that questioned her sanity. "She has nothing to do with your situation. She's a nanny I hired from an agency."

"Did you personally check her out?"

"She adores Hope. She wouldn't have anything to do with the kidnapping."

Despite his words, Terry saw fear and doubt creep into his eyes. She laid a hand on his arm. "You're probably right but we can't afford to ignore any possibility."

"Of course not." He turned away, his tone irritable.

His reaction made Terry wonder if there was more

to his relationship with the nanny than being her employer. "Maybe we're looking at this from the wrong angle. Surely you've made your share of enemies because of your job."

He gave a short, derisive laugh. "That's an understatement."

"Well?" she asked, after he'd let a long, tense silence lapse.

"I'm thinking."

Terry wrapped her arms around herself. Not that she thought it would help the knots cramping her stomach, but because Mitch's expression gave her such an uneasy feeling she didn't know what to do. He wasn't just thinking. She could tell a possibility had occurred to him. But he obviously was unwilling to share it with her.

"Maybe we should call the police."

"No." He glared at her. "No police. They'll screw things up."

"What about your FBI friends?"

He stared at her but she knew he was barely listening, and then he abruptly snatched the kidnapper's note and headed out of the nursery.

She hurried after him. "What are you doing?"

He didn't answer, but flipped on a light as he entered a room that looked like it might be his study.

"Mitch?"

He sat at a massive polished cherry desk and opened the top drawer.

"Damn it, Mitch. What's going on?"

"I don't know," he said, shaking his head and staring at a piece of paper he'd withdrawn. His expression was grim, his voice uncertain. "I may be crazy but—" exhaling, he shook his head and handed her the paper "—does any of this mean anything to you?"

She looked at the typed page. It was Margaret Turner's résumé.

Turner?

It couldn't be....

Terry squinted at the sharp pain that pricked the area between her eyes. The dawn of a headache was the least of her worries. So was the rash of goose bumps invading her skin. According to the résumé, Margaret Turner attended Northwestern University the same time Terry had ten years ago.

Meg was also short for Margaret.

"This can't be," she said, shaking her head with denial.

"What?"

"Turner is a common name."

Mitch bolted out of his chair. "You know her?"

Terry's heart slammed against her chest. The paper shook in her hand. "I don't know. I—" She kept shaking her head. "I don't know."

"Okay." He took her by the shoulders, guided her to a chair and sat her down. "Tell me everything."

"It could be a coincidence that this woman went to Northwestern the same time I did. If she really is Meg, surely she wouldn't have given you a truthful résumé."

"Meg?" He ran a soothing hand up and down her arm. "Who's Meg?"

"A woman who went to school with me, and whom I later hired to work at All That Glitters."

"Go on." He sat on the edge of the desk and gently squeezed her arm. "Does she still work for you? What does she do? Tell me everything."

"My sister said she disappeared a month ago." Terry swallowed. "Meg's being investigated regarding the embezzlement case."

He stood, his curse succinct.

"But we always got along. There's no reason she would be involved with any of this. She was happy working at All That Glitters. She loved living in Rio."

He'd moved with restless energy to the window, but turned suddenly. "Wait a minute. You used to watch Hope at the park. She was with Margaret. You would have recognized her."

Terry wished it were true. "I was always too far away. I only saw that the woman had dark, kind of wild hair. Meg kept hers in a tight bun. I couldn't even tell you how long it was."

She thought for a moment. "Meg was always a little heavier, more round in the hip area. And shy. Quiet. I'd say even a little timid."

"You don't think she could be the same person?"

It was obvious he thought so. Terry moistened her dry lips. "It's certainly possible."

"I'll have her passport checked." He pulled out his cell phone. "See if she's left Rio."

Terry picked up the résumé again. She and Meg had never been close. They'd shared one mutual acquaintance in school and were in several classes together, but they hung around different crowds. In fact, Terry couldn't recall any one specific friend Meg hung around with. She was always sort of *there*.

But Terry had known and liked her enough to hire her when the woman had shown up unexpectedly in Rio. Meg certainly had been a competent bookkeeper. In fact, if anything, she was overqualified. People who graduated from a college like Northwestern didn't usually end up as bookkeepers. But Terry hadn't thought much about that since Meg was so shy and not the ambitious sort.

Forcing herself to remember, she continued to scan the résumé, thinking back on everything she could recall about Meg. The place of birth, age, educational history—everything matched. Except for her employment over the past ten years. Margaret Turner had worked as a nanny for an American diplomat abroad.

"I have someone working on the passport."

At the sound of Mitch's voice, she looked up. "When she calls back, I'm going to tell her I know who she is."

He studied her a moment, and then glanced at the résumé she still held. "Something there convince you?"

"It'll sound odd."

He snorted. "I've heard it all."

She paused, wondering how to phrase her suspicion. There was no easy way to explain. "Sometimes I used to feel uneasy around her. I can't tell you why exactly, but it was almost as though she tried too hard to get my attention at times." She shrugged. "For a while, in college, I thought she was gay. But it wasn't that, it was more like a little sister wanting to hang around a big sister and her friends. Some of the other girls used to tease me that I had a fan.''

Mitch's face darkened, his gaze drifting off, his lips pulled in a grim line.

"But that was only for a few months during our junior year when I first met her. That was more than ten years ago, and she's been fine since, or I wouldn't have hired her.''

He nodded slowly. ''And then she followed you to Rio,'' he said almost to himself.

"She showed up six months after graduation. Why are you looking like that?''

He started punching in numbers on his cell phone.

''Mitch? What?''

With a grunt of disgust, he disconnected the call. But he promptly pressed redial.

''Mitch, don't do this to me.''

He looked up, perplexed, as though he hadn't heard her the first time.

"You have to tell me what you're thinking, what action you think we should take.'' She remained calm when she really wanted to scream. "You're used to this. I'm not. Shut me out and I'll go crazy.''

Anger sparked in his eyes. ''I'm used to this? She's my daughter, for God's sakes.''

"I know. But she's my daughter, too, and I have to know what's going on.''

Mitch briefly closed his eyes and exhaled, strain and anguish lining his face. ''You're right. I'm sorry.''

She laid a hand over his much larger one. He

turned it over so that their palms met and he squeezed gently. "What do you think she'll do next?"

"She'll call back soon. She wants us to squirm, but she won't be able to resist hearing our reaction. Of course, we're assuming a lot here."

"That it's Meg?" Terry shivered. "It's her. I know it. Call it a mother's intuition or whatever you want, but I know it's her."

"I think you're right. The pieces fit. She was able to control some of her behavior in the beginning, but the pattern of obsession is there."

"I feel so stupid."

"Don't." He let go of her hand and slid an arm around her. "It's only easy to see in retrospect."

"That's the thing. I keep replaying incidents that I found strange at the time, but brushed off. If I had only—"

"Shh." He put a finger to her lips. "If you start second-guessing yourself, you will go crazy and you won't be any help to me or Hope. Forget about what you think you should've done. Until now you didn't understand the game or her twisted rules."

Terry shrugged away from his comforting arm. Easy for him to say. This was her fault. She should have been more astute, more mindful of Meg's sometimes odd behavior, instead of dismissing it as an occasional personality quirk.

She paced to the window, her arms crossed as she rubbed the sudden chill from them. When she turned back, Mitch was studying her with concern in his eyes. She took a deep breath, relaxed her arms. "I want the truth. Will she hurt Hope Katherine?"

"I don't think so," he said, slowly shaking his head, his gaze holding hers. "It's you she wants."

Terry blinked. "Me?"

"I'd bet my career on it."

"But why go through all this trouble? We worked four offices away for ten years."

"What color are her eyes?"

That startled a nervous laugh out of her. "What are you—"

"Tell me what color they are."

She shrugged, searched her memory. "Green. No...brown. What difference does it make?"

"What kind of car does she drive?"

"How would I know?"

"What's her favorite type of food?"

"Mitch...what the hell is wrong with you?"

He looked dead serious. "Can you answer any of those questions?"

She waved her hand in exasperation. "No."

"But you worked with her all these years."

"In the same office, yes." Terry had a horrible feeling she knew where he was going with this. "But that doesn't mean we traveled in the same social circle."

"Don't sound so defensive. I'm not sure I could answer those questions about guys I've worked with. But none of them were so obsessed with me, they'd do anything to get my attention."

Oh, God, Terry wanted to sit down and cry. She'd barely had the time of day for the woman. "You think she just wants my attention?"

He scrubbed at his face and sighed. "It's more than that at this point. My guess is she wants to be you."

"I'm not sure I follow."

"She wants you out of the picture, so she can slip into your life. That's why I don't believe she'll harm Hope. By now, she may even have convinced herself Hope is her daughter."

"This is so bizarre." She stared at Mitch, seeing him in a new light. How did he do it? This was a big part of his job...analyzing twisted minds, having to explain to ordinary people why their lives suddenly had been turned upside down by a sick person's greed or vengeance.

He was a good man. He didn't deserve to be thrown into this mess. Not that she could do anything about it now. But she'd been a different person when she first met Meg. Totally self-absorbed, Terry had been so sure the entire world was watching her, waiting for her to screw up.

When she'd occasionally let down her guard, her father was quick to remind her how disappointed he was in not having a son to take over the business. He'd expected so little from Terry, even when she gave a thousand percent. Even when she'd increased profits over and above what anyone had anticipated. Nothing she did was ever good enough for him.

Mitch would never be that kind of father. He'd nurture Hope Katherine's spirit, encourage her sense of adventure and accept her choices.

Terry's breath shuddered in her chest.

But first, they had to get her baby back.

"Terry?"

She snapped out of her preoccupation.

"I'm not sure you fully understand." He paused, trapping her gaze, certain he had her full attention. "Margaret Turner probably wants you dead."

She took a deep breath, and then nodded slowly.

Mitch watched her face pale, noticed how she tried to hide her shaky hands. Helplessness burned a hole in his gut. He felt like punching a wall. Hell of a lot of good that would do.

"I'm not trying to scare you," he continued. "I want you to understand what we're up against."

"I understand fully. When Meg calls, we offer her a deal. Me in exchange for Hope Katherine."

His heart thudded at the brave way she lifted her chin, the lack of hesitation in offering herself. Steely determination flashed in her eyes. He admired her grit, but he was going to have to get past it.

"That won't happen." He put up a silencing hand as soon as she opened her mouth to protest. "You have to trust me. It isn't that simple."

"You said yourself that it's me she wants."

"Yeah, but she also wants to see you suffer first. I think we can safely guess she was the one who set you up for embezzlement, and probably the smuggling charge."

"How could she possibly manage to do all that?"

"I don't know. But that's my best guess. If she just wanted to see you dead, she would have hidden in a dark alley and popped you one night." He tried to ignore the way she flinched at his words. This was ugly business. She needed thick skin if they were going to get Hope back. "She wants to see you squirm.

She felt rebuffed. It was painful for her. She feels she owes you in kind.''

Terry closed her eyes for a moment. When she opened them again, the pain he saw there staggered him. ''It's not fair,'' she whispered. ''Hope Katherine is innocent. If her mother hadn't been such a self-centered, egotistical—''

''We can both blame ourselves. It won't help.''

Her eyes widened. There was loathing in their depths. Not directed at him, but at herself. ''You're not to blame. I'm not a child. I don't need you to soften the consequences of my selfish actions.''

He shook his head. ''You weren't trained in criminal psychology. It would be easy for you to dismiss strange behavior. I'm the one who should have picked up on Margaret's oddities, even the way she cooed to Hope in Portuguese. Look at the way the house is even decorated Rio-style. That was her influence and I never questioned her. Believe me, at this point, she probably wants to see me squirm almost as much as you.''

Terry's gaze narrowed in question. ''Why?''

''In a way, I rebuffed her, too.''

''She came on to you?''

Mitch rotated his shoulder, an involuntary nervous reaction he detested. ''Sort of. I didn't see it myself, but some of my friends thought she was…interested. In retrospect, the attraction had to do with you. She perceived me as something of yours, so she wanted me.''

''But how could she have known about you?'' Her cheeks turned slightly pink. ''I may have said something to my sister about meeting you, but certainly nothing to Meg.''

"She found out you had a baby. You brought the baby here to me. Wouldn't be hard for her to figure out our connection.''

Terry blanched. "You think she's been following me all along.''

"No, but if she was in on the smuggling setup, that would mean she knew Leo Hayes. I'm sure he provided her with a hell of a lot of information before he died.''

"That's a lot of supposition. I guess we may never know for sure.''

"We will when we catch her.''

"Will we?'' Terry's bleak stare dared him to lie.

He nodded. "Yes. But we have to work together. No more sniping at each other.''

"Agreed.''

"And when she calls—''

The shrill ring of the phone cut him off.

CHAPTER SIX

MITCH GOT to the phone first. He was surprised she'd call back so quickly...assuming it was Margaret. Hoping like hell he was mentally prepared to act objectively, he picked up the receiver.

"Barnes," he answered.

The strange garbled voice was on the other end. But this time, as he listened carefully, it was easier to tell it belonged to a woman. She obviously wasn't using any type of sophisticated scrambling device, more likely a piece of cloth muffling the phone.

"Have you missed her?" the caller asked.

"Tell us what you want." Mitch shared the earpiece of the receiver with Terry when she moved in close.

"I give the orders." The voice was harsh, desperate.

"Of course. We're simply waiting for you to tell us what to do."

"It's not fun waiting, is it?"

Terry opened her mouth to respond, but he gave a firm shake of his head and yanked the phone away.

"I'm talking to you." The voice got shriller. "It's not fun having to wait, is it?"

"No."

"Tell me how it feels."

Terry made a sign she'd keep her mouth shut, and he brought the phone back within hearing distance before he said, "We need to know if Hope is all right."

A string of obscenities filled the phone line. "What kind of monster do you think I am?"

He gave Terry a warning look. "What about Margaret, her nanny, is she okay, too?"

The woman's hysterical laughter grated on his ears. "You're both so stupid. You're the worst kind of fools, thinking you're smarter and better than everyone else, when you really don't know a damn thing."

"Tell us what you want," Mitch said in a low, soothing voice. "And we'll do it."

"Damn right you will." She paused, her breathing labored.

"How does it feel to be out of control? To have someone else pull the strings? It stinks, doesn't it?"

"Yeah, it stinks."

"Good. I hope you're both drowning in misery by now, wondering if you'll ever see your precious child again."

Terry closed her eyes and bit her lower lip, her teeth sinking in deep. Mitch rubbed her arm. Her skin was ice-cold. "You've got your wish," he said calmly. "What do we do next?"

"Stop rushing me!"

In the background, Hope began to wail. "What's going on?" He gripped the phone tighter. "Why is she crying?"

"It's your fault. You made me yell and frighten her."

The phone dropped with a deafening clang.

And then faintly, he could hear Margaret trying to console Hope.

Terry looked as though she were about to jump out of her skin. He cupped a hand over the mouthpiece and said, "At least we know Hope is all right."

"Why don't I try to talk to her?" She reached for the phone, but he held it away. "She knows me better. Maybe I can reason with her, offer her money to disappear."

"You know it's not about money, and talking to you may inflame her more. I'll get her to—" He stopped abruptly when he heard the phone on the other end being picked up.

"Listen, I have to feed her. She's hungry." Margaret sounded harried. Not a good sign. "In two hours go to Fifth and Vinyon. There's a bar on the corner. Go inside and you'll receive further instructions."

"Margaret, wait. Don't hang up." Too late, he realized his slip.

After a long pause and more labored breathing, she said, "Very good, Agent Barnes. Now try to catch me."

The line went dead.

THE BAR WAS in one of the seediest parts of town. Parked outside were three brand-new Harleys, a rusted-out pickup truck and a nondescript white sedan with a car rental sticker.

Terry's pulse quickened. If Meg was inside herself,

maybe Terry could reason with her. However, Mitch had warned her not to expect any face-to-face contact. At least not yet. But who around here would drive a rental?

"You want to go inside with me?" Mitch pulled the Ford Explorer into a space behind the Harleys.

"Funny, I was going to ask you the same thing."

He gave her a wry look. "I don't know what kind of place this is. You might be more comfortable staying in the car."

As Terry opened the door and got out, she heard Mitch sigh.

She appreciated that he was trying to protect her. Ironically, he'd be quite surprised at the places she'd had to call home in the past few months. Motel rooms with roaches so big she kept a fly swatter beside her at all times, and doors that had been broken down so many times they couldn't lock. It had been a humbling experience. She'd had no idea people lived that way.

Mitch got to the door of the bar first, and as soon as he opened it the smell of stale smoke and sweat shrouded her senses. Dimly lit, the place smelled like a dirty ashtray, and Terry hoped to God that Meg hadn't brought Hope Katherine in here.

"Change your mind about waiting in the car?" Mitch did nothing to hide his disgust as he surveyed the rust-colored stains on the floor and walls.

"How did she find this place?" she murmured, sidestepping a chair that had been left tipped over.

All four patrons immediately looked up and trained their curious stares on Terry. The paunchy bald guy behind the bar gave her such a once-over it made her skin crawl. A pair of leather-clad biker types turned back to their shots of tequila and game of poker.

Mitch muttered a curse. "This better not be a wild-goose chase."

Although she'd spoken English most of her life, that particular phrase didn't register. But the fact Mitch seemed agitated was enough to make her uneasy. Her gaze was drawn to a man sitting by himself in a booth. It appeared as though he were about to pass out. "No one looks like they would have instructions for us."

"It's gotta be the bartender." Mitch cast a quick glance over his shoulder at the back corners of the room. "Stay close."

She laughed humorlessly to herself. This time he got no argument.

The bald man put both beefy hands on the bar and leaned forward as they approached. His bold gaze stayed on Terry, and as it wandered to her breasts, he suggestively licked his lips.

She felt Mitch's tension mount, saw how he clenched his fists, and she subtly reached for his hand, loosening his fingers and intertwining them with hers.

"It's not worth it," she whispered. "Let's just get Hope Katherine back."

At the mention of their daughter, his grip tightened. She squeezed gently, and then he relaxed, his chest rising and falling with two deep breaths.

Mitch nodded at the man. "I understand you have a message for us."

The bartender didn't even look at Mitch. His eyes stayed on Terry. "How much?"

Mitch frowned, and then he started digging in his pocket. He pulled out some bills and counted them. "All I have on me is seventy-six dollars."

The other guy drew his head back, his scowl causing his forehead to crease clear into his pasty white scalp. "What the hell you trying to pull, buddy boy?"

Mitch snorted. "I assumed you wanted payment for the information."

"Shit!" The guy spat into something behind the bar. "I meant how much for her?"

Terry gasped, and squeezed Mitch's hand tighter. She was about to tell the man to go to hell, but she held her tongue, knowing he might hold the key to finding Hope Katherine.

Anger radiated from Mitch, but he remained admirably calm. "We seem to have a misunderstanding. We were told to come here to receive some instructions."

"Yeah?" The bartender looked from Mitch to Terry.

"A woman in her early thirties," Terry said quickly. "About five-five, brown hair...she was supposed to have left word for us." She forced herself to smile. "It's really important."

"I know who you mean." He grunted. "A real nutcase. Great ass, though."

"She left something?" Unasked, Mitch laid down the money he'd pulled from his pocket.

The guy scratched his chest while he eyed the bills,

and then his gaze went back to Terry. "She said you were for sale."

"That's all?" Mitch cut in before Terry had a chance to respond.

"Maybe." He didn't even look at Mitch but kept staring at Terry, his gaze roaming insolently over her body. "How bad you want that information, babe?"

Mitch reached over the counter and grabbed the bartender's T-shirt, tearing it near the neckband. "I'm going to ask you one more time while I still feel like being polite."

Startled, Terry moved back. This was a new side to Mitch. His voice was dangerously low and the veins were popping from his neck.

The bartender swore viciously and tried to twist away.

Mitch grabbed his arm and the man yelped. Terry couldn't see what Mitch had actually done but the pain on the other man's face said it all.

"You were saying?" Mitch asked with a deadly smile.

"In the corner." The guy swore again and jerked away, rubbing his wrist. "She left something on the table."

"That wasn't so hard, was it?" Mitch stepped back from the bar but it was clear he was poised to attack again if need be. He glanced around at the other men in the room. They'd barely moved, only stared with idle curiosity. "Now, we'll go have a look, and then leave. Peaceful-like. Got a problem with that?"

"Go get your shit and get the hell out of my place." The bartender straightened his shoulders, fingered the tear in his shirt. "And when you talk to that nutcase, tell her to stay the hell away. Any of you show up here again, I'm calling the cops."

"Yeah, right," Mitch muttered as he motioned Terry to precede him.

She didn't hesitate but headed for the back corner. She didn't see anything at first. The tabletops looked as though they hadn't been wiped off in days and ashtrays overflowed with tar-stained cigarette butts.

And then she saw the small piece of white paper, sitting next to a dirty plate.

In sloppy black letters it said, "How does it feel, Ms. High-and-Mighty Monteverde, to be left with crumbs?"

Terry frowned and reread the note while Mitch peered over her shoulder. At his grunt, she looked up at him.

He was staring at the plate. She followed his gaze and took a closer look. The plate was littered with toast crumbs.

Terry turned over the paper. Nothing. She pushed the plate aside. Nothing was concealed beneath it. Her heart thudded. "What is she saying? This doesn't give us any instructions."

That Mitch looked so calm and thoughtful infuriated her.

"Well, we were right," he finally said. "She wants to see you squirm."

"Is that all you have to say?"

At her harsh tone, he met her gaze. "Would you feel better if I got too furious to think straight?"

"Go to hell."

"Too late, sweetheart. I'm already there."

AFTER A LONG silent ride home, Mitch dropped Terry off at his place to wait for the next phone call. He'd barely hung around for a minute before he took the key she gave him and went to her apartment to pick up her things.

They'd decided it was wiser for her to stay at the house until they got Hope back. For his part, he would have liked Terry as far away as possible.

She distracted him, pissed him off and made him miserable in general. Did she think he didn't share the same fears for their daughter? That he wasn't worried sick himself? He'd never felt so helpless in his entire life, and he wasn't doing helpless well.

He was angry that the bartender had given in so easily. Mitch would have loved to rearrange the guy's face, or at least put a couple of dents in his wall. That would have let off some steam. Maybe even clear his head so he'd know what the hell to do next.

Terry wasn't much help. Not that he blamed her. She wasn't trained for this type of situation and she was too personally involved anyway.

Like he wasn't.

He hit the steering wheel with the heel of his hand. What a mess. How could he have hired someone to watch his daughter without doing a thorough investigation? Why had he accepted the agency's recommendation so readily? Had they even sent her? Or had Margaret intercepted his mail, had his phones tapped? Easy enough to do for a clever, unscrupulous private investigator. God, he'd been such a damn fool.

Although Terry hadn't said anything, he wondered if she blamed him. It was hard enough not to blame himself. Maybe it was self-recrimination that made him see accusation in her eyes, hear disgust in her voice. Feel self-loathing so deep it was burning a hole in his gut.

Damn it! Nothing like a crisis to tear a couple apart, especially when they hadn't even established a real relationship yet. He'd seen similar circumstances often in his job. One person reacts or grieves in one way, and the other can't understand why their partner isn't behaving the way they think they should. Bad enough watching as an objective stranger, but being one of the players really stunk.

Made him wonder about his mother and father. What had driven them apart?

Mitch loved his mother, and he thought she'd done a good job as a single parent, but he wasn't ignorant of her shortcomings. She'd had a stubborn streak longer than the Continental Divide, and if it had suited her purpose not to reveal her pregnancy, well, Mitch wasn't so sure she would have been forthright.

If Terry hadn't been desperate for help, Mitch might never have known about Hope. He didn't want to think that—preferred to think that Terry had more integrity than to be so selfish—but the truth was, he didn't know.

Maybe he wasn't being fair to his father. If the man didn't know of Mitch's existence, it was up to Mitch to continue the search for him. Lily Garrett Bishop had been doing some checking for him.

He turned onto Wesson Street and immediately saw the number of the address Terry had given him. The sign was nailed to a one-story building that looked as though it might crumble at any moment. He checked the number again. Sure enough, Terry had been living in this dump.

Man, it was an eyesore. A row of five or six apartments, each door a different color of chipped paint. Hard to imagine her staying there. It was a far cry from the cushy lifestyle she'd been accustomed to all her life. In spite of himself, an arrow of sympathy found its way to his heart as he veered toward the driveway.

Not a single parking space was available so he took an illegal one by the sidewalk. He'd be less than five minutes according to Terry. She traveled light these days. He didn't blame her…anyone would want to get the hell out of here fast.

From his pocket he dug out the key she'd given him and hurried toward the door. He unlocked it, then cast a brief glance over his shoulder at his car. No one was on the street, but it took kids only minutes to swipe hubcaps. He hoped his were still there when he came back.

He'd barely pushed the key into the lock and the door creaked open. What a joke. A piece of masking tape could almost serve the same purpose. No matter what happened, Terry was not coming back here. If she thought she was strong-willed, he'd give her a dose of his own brand of stubborn.

He pushed the door wider. It wasn't an apartment, just a room, like an efficiency. A double bed was in one corner, and across from it a small wet-bar-size refrigerator sat beside a table with a hot plate on it.

After crossing over a faded blue woven rug, he

peeked into a small bathroom with an ancient sink and john. The shower stall was missing a few tiles and most of the grout had peeled away. Nevertheless, the place was spotless, and it smelled faintly of roses—Terry's scent.

His mind immediately started to wander, remembering the feel of her hair on his bare chest, the silky warmth of her olive skin, and he had to force himself to concentrate on taking care of business. All her clothes were neatly folded and it took no time to place them in her suitcase.

The thing was, their attraction hadn't just been physical. They'd talked for hours…about everything. Nothing had been taboo. He'd bared his soul, and she hers. Before the sex. The hottest, most satisfying sex he'd ever had in his life.

But that was precisely what he couldn't think about. The amazingly vivid memories of their one night clouded his judgment, made him long for a life that may not be possible. The memories prevented him from discovering what kind of woman Terry really was.

He looked around again at the dreary furnishings, the faded walls. She'd surprised him once again. He knew money had to have been tight, but this?

She'd spared no expense on Hope, though. Their baby had obviously been well cared for and in perfect health when she was delivered to him. Becoming a father overnight had been his only challenge. He'd learned quickly. Just as Terry must have. But at least he'd had the luxury of safety and comfort while he discovered how to cope with a baby.

He checked the bathroom to make sure he'd collected everything, and then opened the single nightstand drawer. Inside was a file...the detective's report on him. The bill was attached. It was marked paid and the amount was a whopper. That's where a good deal of Terry's money had gone. Again, she'd put Hope first by making sure he had the right stuff to be a father.

Mitch swallowed around the lump in his throat, tucked the file under his arm, and then picked up the suitcase. The temptation to sit down and read it was great, but he had to get back to Terry. He didn't want her to have to wait for the phone call alone. She'd already been through a lot by herself and without a word of complaint. He was starting to figure out that she was some lady.

He turned to leave and caught movement out of the corner of his eye. Before he could react, he saw the baseball bat come out of nowhere. It hit him on the side of his temple.

Pain blistered his senses and he stumbled backward, dropping the suitcase and the file.

And then everything went black.

CHAPTER SEVEN

TERRY HEARD the garage door open and ran to the window. Mitch's Explorer was halfway down the drive. She slumped against the wall and breathed a sigh of relief. He'd been gone way too long. Thank God he was all right. That way she could strangle him herself.

She headed for the kitchen and the door that led to the garage, and then waited with her arms crossed. The noisy garage door creaked as it was lowered, but still Mitch didn't come in. She was about to open the door herself when the knob finally turned.

She stepped back and refolded her arms.

He looked like hell. She narrowed her gaze on his disheveled clothes, his messy hair. Surely he wouldn't have gone to a bar.

"Why didn't you call?" she asked. "I've been worried sick. I even tried your cell phone. Where were you?"

He gave her a blank look.

"Are you drunk?"

He grunted as he set down her suitcase. "No, but it sounds like a hell of an idea."

She frowned at his odd behavior, tightened her

folded arms and hunched her shoulders. It seemed a little chilly all of a sudden. "No phone call yet."

"I know."

"How could you?"

"Margaret decided to use an alternative form of communication." He went to the refrigerator and got ice out of the freezer.

"What are you talking about—" As he turned she saw the swelling near his temple. Some of the skin had already started to bruise. She gasped. "What happened?"

"She must have followed me to your place." He withdrew a folded piece of paper from his pocket and handed it to her.

"I found this when I came to."

Terry unfolded the note, torn between asking him more questions and finding out what the note said. Her gaze quickly scanned the nearly illegible writing. "Don't underestimate me. I'm in complete control. I'll call when I'm good and ready."

"Oh, my God, she is crazy." Crazy enough to hurt their daughter? Mitch was convinced she wouldn't, and Terry needed to hang on to that belief. She looked up. Mitch was wrapping a dish towel around the ice. She doubted it would hold together. "Let me help you with that." She reached for the towel but he evaded her.

"I'm fine."

His curt tone startled her. "I'm sorry I jumped on you as soon as you walked in the door. I was worried."

He glanced at the clock, and then at her. He stared

at her for a long moment, his eyes probing and concerned. "I should have called when I came to. I apologize."

"You're all right. That's the main thing." She squinted at the side of his face. "Maybe you should go to a doctor."

"No way. I've had it with doctors."

"Yeah, but—"

"I'm fine. This isn't the first bump on my noggin, and I doubt it'll be the last."

"What did she use to hit you?"

"A baseball bat."

Terry gasped. "You could have a concussion. Maybe we could get a doctor to come here."

"Look, it hurts like a son of a bitch so if it's all the same to you, would you shut up and give me some peace and quiet."

She blinked. "I'm only trying to help."

"Yeah, I know." Sighing, he sank onto the kitchen chair nearest the window and stared outside while he clutched the towel-wrapped ice to his temple. "I feel like a jerk. It never occurred to me she'd get that close."

"Ah…" Terry nodded, understanding what had caused his dark mood, and took a chair across from him.

He frowned at her. "Ah, what?"

She shook her head, deciding her observation might provoke him. "What's your feeling? Do you think she'll call tonight?"

His gaze lowered to her tightly clutched hands, and she tried to relax them. "Hard to say. She obviously likes making us wait, but she also wants in on the fun of seeing our reaction.''

That told her absolutely nothing. She unfolded her hands, tried to take a couple of deep breaths. "Something else occurred to me. When Meg's running around leaving us notes or following you, where is she leaving Hope Katherine?"

"I wondered about that myself. My guess is that she leaves Hope in the car. I doubt Margaret has involved anyone else. Too risky, for one thing, and since it's not about money, she'd have a hard time convincing some loser to play her way.''

Terry shivered. "I'd almost like to think of our baby being left alone in the car rather than in the clutches of some stranger. Is that terrible?"

A faint smile curved his mouth as he shook his head. "No, that's not terrible. Anybody willing to help a baby kidnapper isn't at the top of my list of caregivers, either.''

"That's my way of thinking." Her gaze wandered toward the phone, her mind willing it to ring.

"I know it's not much consolation, but I firmly believe Margaret won't hurt Hope. Sometimes I'd watch them playing when Margaret didn't know I was around. She genuinely does love Hope. In fact, by now, I wouldn't be surprised if she's convinced herself that Hope is her child.''

Terry shuddered. "What if she takes her away? She could go abroad somewhere and we'd never find her.''

"Not until she's paid you back.''

She let out a pent-up breath and went back to staring at the phone. "Of course."

"Ouch!"

She jerked her gaze to Mitch. He was rubbing his right eye. "What happened?"

"I poked my eye with this damn piece of ice."

She stood. "Give that to me." He gave her a blank look. "Now," she said, and grabbed the damp towel out of his hand.

"What's your problem?" His grumpy tone made her smile a little.

"You." She carried the bunched-up towel to the sink and dumped the ice. "You're my problem. You're being stubborn and it's affecting your common sense."

"I beg your pardon."

"And when your judgment is affected, so am I." She got more ice out of the freezer and filled a small plastic bag with it. Then she wrapped the towel around the plastic bag. "I need you, Agent Barnes. Hope Katherine needs you. Don't allow your ego to let us down."

"My ego?" He stared at her with first surprise, then anger. He didn't even take the ice pack she tried handing him. "What the hell does my ego have to do with this?"

She raised her brows at him.

"Don't give me that haughty look." He tried to snatch the ice pack, but this time she hid it behind her back and moved closer to him.

She squinted down at his injury. "Did you know the skin broke?" She pushed back his hair. "You have a cut that's a half-inch long. You need a couple of stitches."

"I don't need any stitches."

"Did you even look at this?"

"Yeah, I looked at it." He jerked his head away. "Ouch! You're not helping matters."

"I'm calling a doctor."

"No, you aren't." He grabbed her wrist when she started to move away. "I don't need one. This is no big deal."

"But you—"

"Terry, for God's sake, I've been shot twice, bitten by a German shepherd, grazed by a butcher knife, and for an encore, screwed up my Achilles tendon. I think I'll live."

She stiffened, recalling the scar she'd found on his thigh the night she explored his body. She'd made him tell her how he'd gotten it—from a bullet he'd taken during a crack house raid—and she'd kissed it, then trailed her lips to his groin, and did something she'd never before done.

Her pulse quickened at the memory and her blood grew warm. It had truly been an amazing night....

"Terry?"

She blinked, and then met his worried gaze. "Yes?"

"Are you all right?"

"Of course." She brought up the ice pack and placed it on his head.

"Ouch!"

"Don't be a baby."

He snorted. "First I'm being foolish by not going

to the doctor, and then I'm a baby because I react when you conk me with the ice pack?''

"I didn't conk you." She scowled at him. "What is 'conk'?''

"It means clobber, smack."

She waved her hand in exasperation. "I did no such thing. Here. Hold on to this."

The corners of his mouth turned up and he relaxed in his chair. "I kind of like you holding it for me."

"Too bad." She waited a moment but he didn't move. "I swear I'll drop it."

"No, you won't."

"Mitch…" She drew his name out in warning, but still he made no move to take over the ice pack.

He smiled up at her, his eyes so damn blue and tempting, she did want to conk him. "You make a terrific nurse."

"You need a doctor." She lifted her chin. "A psychiatrist."

"Probably."

"I'm letting go of the ice pack now."

"No, you're not." He slid an arm around her waist and drew her closer.

His warm breath brushed the skin where her blouse dipped in a V. "Don't be so sure of yourself, Mitch."

"I'm not." He gave her such a sexy yet sweet smile, her heart thudded. "I'm sure of you."

She nearly dropped the ice. "Don't be." And then she did drop it. Deliberately.

He released her and made a grab for the loosened towel and ice bag as they fell. When he moaned in pain, regret subdued her irritation. Although why he'd upset her she wasn't sure. Maybe because he thought he had her figured out. Even what he thought he knew about her was no longer true. A lot had happened during the past year. She wasn't the same woman she'd been when she first met him. A fact she didn't regret.

"What the hell did you do that for?" He retrieved the towel and most of the ice. The rest had slid across the floor. Ignoring the strays, he straightened.

"Oh, you're bleeding again." Shame heated her face as she pushed his hair aside. "Let me tend to it."

He reared back. "Forget it. I'll look after it myself."

"I'm sorry for dropping the ice. That was childish. Now, please, let me help."

He gave her a resentful glare, and then sighed, his shoulders drooping. "All right."

Terry took a deep breath. He'd been through a lot today. They both had. It wouldn't kill her to be kinder to him, to give him the benefit of the doubt instead of making wild assumptions.

"Where are your first-aid supplies?"

"In my bathroom. The last door down the hall."

"I'll be right back."

Mitch hesitated a moment, wondering what kind of shape he'd left his bedroom in. God knew what he'd left lying around. "I'll go with you."

She stopped at the door and glanced back at him. "Why?"

"Because I'm tired of sitting in the kitchen."

She frowned, suspicion drawing her brows together.

"Okay, you caught me." It took some effort for him to raise himself from the chair. "I just want to get you in my bed."

"Like hell..."

He laughed, and then scowled. "Ouch!"

"If you're looking for sympathy—"

"I'm not looking for a damn thing." His tone was sharp but he'd gotten light-headed all of a sudden and had to hold the counter for support.

She sighed and backtracked toward him. "Come here."

"Just go." He gestured with his hand. "I'm right behind you."

She gave him a placating smile, and then slipped an arm around his waist. "Lean on me."

He was tempted to refuse, but the soft curves of her body were an even greater temptation and he let himself relax against her. "Let it be known I'm not as stubborn as you think."

Her soft laughter filled his senses and warmed all the cold empty places in his soul. Just like it had the night they met.

As dangerous as it was to hang on to the memories, the greater danger to him was the accuracy of his recollection. It would've been easier if his musings had surpassed reality.

They continued on to his room in silence and he was relieved to see he hadn't left the place in too big a mess. Although the bed wasn't made, he'd pulled the quilt up to the pillows. Good enough for a day he didn't have to change the sheets.

"Why don't you sit on the bed while I go see what I can find in your medicine cabinet?" Terry looked up at him, her eyes warm and concerned.

All he could do was nod, and sink to the edge of the mattress. She hesitated, pushing his hair aside and staring at his injury, and he had the overwhelming desire to wrap his arms around her and bury his face in her soft breasts.

She probed the wounded area, her fingers gentle and soothing. "You need to keep ice on the swelling. After I clean out this cut, I'll go make a fresh pack."

"Maybe I should go make it while you—"

She put a finger to his lips. "You are going to stay right here. Understand?"

He smiled, and she quickly pulled her finger away. "Yes, ma'am."

"I mean it."

"I know."

She took another look at his injury, gave him a warning look and then headed for the bathroom.

He watched the slight sway of her hips, the way her hair shimmered in even the least amount of light, how her shoulders squared, her back strong and straight. She was really something…incredibly feminine and sensual without lifting a finger, yet possessing the inner strength of steel.

Her father was so damn wrong about her. Mitch wished she could see it as clearly as he could. The night she told him about the struggle with her father, how he'd never once given her his approval no matter what she achieved, Mitch had experienced her hurt so acutely it could have been his own.

That she hadn't complained, but spoke matter-of-factly, made the pain all the more poignant. But she hadn't fooled him. Her father's disappointment wounded her to her core. And all because she hadn't been born a son.

"I wish you were better equipped," she said, returning with a frown and her hands full. "You really should have a good antiseptic. The only one I found is expired."

Mitch smiled. He couldn't help it. She sounded so maternal. Very unlike the woman in Lily Garrett Bishop's preliminary report.

She narrowed her gaze. "Why are you smiling at me like that?"

He shrugged. "I just remembered that there's more stuff in the guest bathroom. Margaret kept it stocked for Hope."

At the mention of Margaret, Terry flinched, and he wanted to kick himself for bringing up the woman. Not that the situation was ever far from either of their minds, but he didn't want to rob Terry of even a moment's respite from worrying.

She visibly swallowed. "I'll go check. Stay put."

"Terry, wait."

She left the room without a backward glance.

Mitch rubbed his jaw. Even the slight movement hurt his head. Damn that Margaret. What the hell was she up to? Had there been a reason to try to disable him? Was this more of her cruel baiting, or was she trying to get him out of the picture to make Terry more vulnerable? That possibility concerned him.

He'd certainly think twice about the two of them being separated again. Terry was going to have to stick close whether she liked it or not. She'd give him a hassle, but tough. He didn't think he'd share his suspicion with her. Knowing how stubborn she was, she'd probably welcome the opportunity to meet Margaret face-to-face and alone.

In fact, where the heck was Terry? She'd been gone too long. Tempted as he was to lie back on the inviting mattress, he pushed himself to his feet and moved gingerly toward the bathroom midway down the hall.

She was still in there, leaning against the wall, tracing her fingers over Hope's favorite bath toy, an ugly rubber duck.

On her face was a faraway look, and a sad, sweet smile lifted her lips slightly. Her shoulders, however, were hunched in defeat. What the hell had he done bringing Margaret into his home?

"Did you find what you were looking for?"

At the sound of his voice, she looked up, startled, the haunted expression on her face breaking his heart again. Quickly she set the duck back in the corner of the tub. "You were right. The cabinet is well-stocked. I'll just be a minute longer."

"Terry?"

She wouldn't look at him again. "Go back and sit down."

"Terry, it's okay to show you're hurting. You don't have to be strong all the time."

She brought down the ointment and extra large bandages. "I'd really appreciate it if you'd get off your feet. I don't fancy having to carry you back."

He chuckled. "You and what football team?"

She frowned. "American humor? Or is that your ego talking?"

He sighed. "Let's go."

"I said I'd only be a minute."

"Problem is, I think I need a little assistance here." He leaned heavily against the wall for good measure. Just in case she saw through his lie.

She immediately abandoned the supplies and went to his side. "Here," she said, slipping an arm around him.

"Don't forget the stuff."

"I'll come back for it."

He groaned. "Terry."

She stared up at him and opened her mouth to speak, but then shook her head and collected the first-aid supplies. When she brought her arm back around him, he leaned into her, enjoying her closeness and feeling not one bit guilty he'd lied about needing her help. Right now, they needed each other's comfort.

When they were back in his room, she immediately got busy cleaning the wound. Each time he tensed at the stinging, she laid a warm, soothing hand on his arm. Her breasts met him eye level and he stared at them, remembering the feel of them in his hands, the taste of them on his tongue. There was no better pain reliever.

She started to unwrap a bandage and he stopped her.

"In the side drawer of my desk is some glue. Mind getting it?"

"Glue?" She made a face. "What for?"

"To close up that cut."

Her eyes widened. "Are you insane?"

"It's worked twice before."

"You can't be serious."

"Actually, a doctor friend of mine gave me the tip." Mitch gently probed the area around the cut. Yup, less than an inch. "Of course he'd prefer stitches, but in an emergency, this will work."

"This isn't an emergency. You could go to the doctor if you weren't so stubborn."

"You're right. I'm hardheaded. Now will you get the glue or should I?"

"Don't you dare move." She gave him a scolding glare before she disappeared.

This time she was back in seconds, the smooth skin between her brows furrowed as she stared at the tube of glue. "How do I do this?"

"Just pinch the skin together over the wound and slap some glue on it. You'll have to hold it for about a minute until it dries."

She shook her head. "I don't like this."

"I'll do it." He started to rise, but she pushed him back down.

"No, I mean I don't like any of this. It'll probably give you an infection."

"Not if you hold the skin together tightly enough. None of the glue will get in the wound." He watched doubt and concern cloud her face. "Look, I understand. I'll do it, but I need a mirror."

"Sit." She glared at him when he started to get up again, and then she wiped her palm on her skirt, took a deep breath and uncapped the glue.

He kept perfectly still while she worked. Only his heart beat faster than normal. She was worried and nervous and it had to do with not wanting to hurt him. That thought alone did him more good than any kind of medicine.

"You okay?" she asked.

"Fine."

"I'm waiting for it to dry."

"Uh-huh." He stared at her breasts again, amazed to find that he was actually getting hard.

"It's been forty seconds. I'll give it another twenty."

"What?"

"The glue…it's almost bonding. I sure hope you know what you're talking about. I've never heard of such a thing."

"It'll be fine," he muttered, not entirely sure what she'd said. Her breasts seemed fuller, rounder than he remembered.

"Okay, that should do it." She took a step back, but he circled his arms around her and she froze.

"Thanks, honey."

She blinked, stiffened a little and mumbled something in Portuguese.

He smiled. "No fair. I don't understand."

She put a tentative hand on his shoulder, her almond-shaped eyes glowing with awareness. "Good."

Running a hand down her back, he urged her closer. Uncertainty flickered in her face but she moved in between his spread legs and placed her other hand on his shoulder. He stretched up and kissed the side of her jaw.

Her eyes briefly drifted closed, and he could almost feel the tension drain out of her body. He gathered her closer, ignoring the ache at his temple, and trailed more kisses along her jaw, to her ear. If only he could get her to relax, maybe even get some sleep....

She moved closer still so that the soft pillow of her breasts pressed against his upper chest. The ache at his temple had become a relentless pounding, but he continued to rub her back, massage her loosening muscles.

He looked up into her unfocused eyes, and she lowered her head, her lips slightly parted.

He really wanted to kiss her, but... "Sweetheart?"

She blinked. And then she blinked again, and stiffened. A look of horrified dawning crossed her face and she stepped away, staring at him as if he were the devil himself.

Her hand shot back to slap him.

He caught it a second before she made contact.

CHAPTER EIGHT

"HOW COULD YOU?" Furious, she tried to jerk out of his grasp, but he held firm.

"What's the matter with you?"

"Me?" Her breathing came so quickly she knew she had to gain control of herself or she'd start hyperventilating. "My daughter has been kidnapped and you're thinking about sex?"

The confusion in his expression instantly changed to rage. He let her go with a harsh flick of his wrist. The movement made him grimace, and then the anger was back in his face. "*Your* daughter?"

She lifted her chin and rubbed the area around the wrist he'd held so tightly. Damn him. How could she have allowed herself to be seduced at a time like this? How could she have wanted to—

"Lady, you sure have selective memory." His skin was ashen and his breathing wasn't any better than hers, except she knew it was from pain.

A pang of regret stole her fire. "I'm sorry. I shouldn't have tried to strike you."

"There are a lot of things you shouldn't have done." He really was pale, with beads of sweat forming above his lip.

"Mitch…" She put a hand out but he jerked away. "I was upset about Hope Katherine. I'm so sorry."

"And I'm not upset? Who do you think has been feeding her for the past four months? Bathing her, rushing her to the doctor when her temperature rose one stinking degree? She's every bit my daughter, too, in every sense of the word." His eyes glittered with anger. "And I'm not planning on going anywhere just because you waltzed back into the picture."

She swallowed. Was she facing a custody battle? Oh, God, she couldn't think about that right now. "Mitch, please. I didn't mean anything. I automatically said my daughter." She slowly lifted a shoulder. "I'm not used to thinking in terms of 'we.'"

He seemed to relax but anger still lingered in the tightness of his jaw, the steely blue of his eyes.

"I knew you'd give her the very best care. I trusted you."

His expression softened. Unconsciously he touched a finger to his injury. "Let's forget it. It's a tough time and we're bound to say things we regret."

She nodded, relief filling her until tears threatened. "How about some aspirin?"

"I'll get it." He started to raise himself from the bed.

She blocked his way. "I thought you said we could forget it."

He frowned. "Your point is?"

"Let me get the aspirin for you," she said softly. "You wouldn't have argued five minutes ago."

He eyed her with annoyance and then gave a gruff nod.

She half smiled and quickly got a glass of water out of his bathroom. She'd already brought aspirin with the first-aid things and offered two tablets to him along with the water. Her heart sank when he reached for them but looked as though he was loath to touch her.

"You shouldn't fall asleep," she said, "in case you have a concussion. What can I do to help keep you awake?"

He snorted.

Dare she ask him what *that* meant? "How about something to eat?"

"No, thanks." He drew his legs up onto the bed and dragged his body back toward the headboard.

She hurried to fluff the pillows.

"What are you doing?" He eyed her with suspicion.

"Being nice...and apologetic."

"I thought we agreed to forget it."

She sighed and gave the pillow an extra punch.

"Come here."

Terry slanted him a glance.

He patted the mattress beside him. "I know you won't leave me in peace so you might as well be comfortable."

She started to shake her head.

"For God's sake, there is no hidden agenda here."

"I know that." She shoved back her hair, irritation simmering to the surface. "I'm afraid I'll fall asleep."

"And that would be bad?"

She stared at him. Had he lost his mind? "I have to keep you awake, number one. And if Meg should call—"

"You'd hear the phone ring."

"But I can't."

"Why? Do you think getting some rest, which would be the commonsense thing to do, would make you a bad mother?"

She stiffened. "You say to forget it, but you can't let go, can you?"

A sad smile lifted the corners of his mouth as he slowly shook his head in denial. "I'm trying to keep you from being so hard on yourself. There is nothing we can do but wait. In the meantime, the better rested we are, the clearer our heads."

"That isn't so easy."

"You're right."

Her gaze strayed out the window. Not that she could see anything but the beam of a streetlight. On the other hand, anyone outside had a clear view of what was happening in Mitch's room.

She hurried to close the patterned burgundy drapes, a creepy feeling slinking over her flesh. Meg could be out there watching them. The thought made Terry feel sick to her stomach as she returned to the edge of the bed.

"What's wrong?"

She kept her back to him. "It got dark so fast. I hadn't realized how late it was."

"Not late enough. It's going to be a long night."

She nodded, and then took a deep breath. "She should have asked us to bring some of Hope Katherine's homemade baby food.'' After a brief pause, she added, ''When we went to the bar.''

''I thought of that.'' Mitch shifted his weight, causing the mattress to move. ''I checked the fridge. She took two days' worth of food with her.''

''Two days?'' Terry turned to him. ''What do you think that means?''

He was watching her with an intensity that should have frightened her. It felt oddly reassuring. ''She thinks she'll get what she wants by then.''

''That's good, right? I mean, she can't keep making us wait if she has a deadline in her head.''

A strange expression crossed his face, and he took a moment before he responded. ''I won't lie to you. She's crazy…there's no second-guessing her. If she's enjoying the game too much, there's no telling how long she'll keep us dangling. On the other hand, I feel certain she won't hurt Hope.''

''You said you wouldn't lie to me.'' Terry ripped the thread out she'd been picking at. She had the sudden urge to tear her entire shirt seam. ''How can you be sure she won't hurt our baby?''

''Obviously I can't be certain, but like I said, she's probably convinced Hope belongs to her.''

''But if she's crazy—''

He put out a hand. She hesitated at first, but then crawled to the empty spot beside him, stretched out and stared at the ceiling. When he wrapped his hand around hers, she didn't complain, but soaked up his warmth, gathered comfort from his slightly callused palm.

''You've got to stop it, Terry, or you'll be as crazy

as she is. Believe Hope is fine and well cared for until we have her safely with us again.''

She closed her eyes. He was right, of course, but it was just so damn hard. How did he do it? Even though it was a job and not personal for him, he still had to watch families cope with loss and grief and self-reproach. Watch them get torn apart because they felt so damn helpless.

She knew that kidnapping and missing persons weren't the only aspects of his job. In fact, those types of cases were infrequently assigned to him. But she instinctively knew he was good at handling them. He'd bring peace and order to the chaos, and comfort the fearful loved ones.

But at what cost to him?

She sincerely hoped he thought long and hard about returning to the Bureau. For Hope Katherine's sake. For his own.

"Hey." He squeezed her hand. "You're quiet."

"Nice change, huh?"

He chuckled. "Want me to turn the lamp off?"

"No, I don't want you dozing off on me. How's your head?"

"As hard as ever."

She smiled up at the ceiling. If she turned to look at him, she knew what she'd find—a twinkle in his eye, a lazy curve of his lips. He had nice lips, too. Full and entirely too kissable.

"Hey, Terry…"

"Hmm?"

"How about we pull the quilt over us?"

She propped herself up on her elbows and looked over at him. "Are you chilled?"

"Don't get excited. I'm not cold or feverish or anything else. I just figured we'd be more comfortable." And then he added quickly, "No hidden agenda, either."

"I know." Smiling, she lay down again, rearranging the pillow until it was just right. "You're simply trying to get me to go to sleep."

"Would I be so manipulative?"

She heard the grin in his voice. "Yes, but it won't work. I'm not the least bit tired."

Not when I don't know if my baby has a safe, warm place to sleep.

She squeezed her eyes shut against the sudden destructive thought. Meg was taking good care of Hope Katherine. Terry had to believe that.

She heard the soft beginnings of a snore and her gaze flew to Mitch. His eyes were closed, his jaw relaxed.

"Hey." She gave his arm a gentle shove. "Mitch?"

He didn't open his eyes, but the right corner of his mouth twitched.

"Very funny." She settled back down, this time a tad closer to him. His presence felt warm and comforting.

"Did you want something?"

"Grow up."

He chuckled. "Never."

She rolled her eyes, and then stared at the ceiling again. "Next time I'll give you more than a little shake."

He made a sound of good-natured disbelief.

Silence lapsed and Terry did her best to force her thoughts away from Hope Katherine. The lamp's lightbulb was of a low wattage and cast a soft glow in the room. Enough that she could see how sparsely he'd decorated his bedroom.

While the nursery was bright and cheerful with lots of cute little accessories and accent pieces, his room had only the basic necessities—an armoire, one night-stand with a lamp, a phone, an alarm clock and some loose change on it, and a valet cloaked with a shirt and sport coat. Not even a picture hung on the wall.

If it weren't for the rest of the house, it would seem that he considered the place temporary. He'd only recently moved in. Maybe the explanation was that simple. But she couldn't help but wonder if this had to do with the crossroads he faced with his job. There was still so much she didn't know about him. So very much she wanted to know. Later, she hoped he'd give her the opportunity.

He hadn't made a sound for the past few minutes, and she slowly, quietly turned her head to see if he'd fallen asleep. Quite the contrary. His gaze was on the digital clock, his expression so tense he looked ready to pounce.

The damn fraud.

Here he'd been trying to get her to relax and not worry, and he was as wired as a circuit board.

MITCH STAYED AS QUIET as possible, hardly daring to even glance at Terry. It had taken her so damn long to fall asleep, he'd begun to think it would never happen. Except he knew she was exhausted. So was he. But sleep wouldn't come for him. Adrenaline raged through him like an out of control wildfire.

Was he wrong in deciding to handle this by himself? He didn't have to get the Bureau involved, but he did have friends, like Ernie, who would step in to help in an unofficial capacity. And keep their mouths shut.

Maybe Terry was right. Maybe he *was* too emotionally involved. But damn it, Margaret was crafty and she knew his routine too well. If she smelled interference, no telling what she might do.

God help him, he hoped he was right, but in his gut, he felt keeping the situation contained was the way to go. For Margaret, this was about punishing Terry…and him to a lesser degree. As long as they remained the key players, Margaret wouldn't get spooked. She'd be too wrapped up in the game.

His thoughts started to wander to Hope and he took his own advice and forced them in a different direction. He had to stay as emotionally detached as possible. His daughter's life depended on it.

Beside him, Terry shifted, then snuggled closer. He slowly moved his arm to accommodate her, readjusted the pillow he'd propped up against the headboard. In the short time she'd been asleep, she'd had fitful dreams. It was obvious in her soft plaintive moans, the way her body jerked and twitched.

God, but he wanted to comfort her. Chase away the nightmares and demons. Promise to keep her and Hope safe forever. It was crazy. One minute he was ready to do anything to protect her, and the next he wished she'd disappear and he never had to lay eyes on her again.

"Mitch?" Her voice was sleepy, uncertain.

"Yeah, I'm here." He'd turned off the lamp earlier, throwing the room into darkness.

She yawned. "I think I dozed off for a few minutes."

He smiled. More like four hours. "Try to go back to sleep."

"You didn't sleep, did you?" She pushed herself up to a half-sitting position.

"Not a wink." He coaxed her back down by putting an arm around her and tugging her closer.

She yawned again and curled up, facing him. "Some nurse I turned out to be."

"You hear me complaining?"

"You were probably glad for the peace and quiet."

"Like I said, hear me complaining?"

She gave him a light jab in the arm, and he grunted. "Funny. Can I get you anything?"

"A new head."

"Why? Is that one too fat?"

"Now look who's being funny."

She sighed. "It still hurts?"

"Only when I breathe."

"Would you be serious for a minute?"

"Sweetheart, I'm being very serious."

"Then I must insist you go to the doctor." She started to get up. He tugged her back down.

"Relax. I'm not going anywhere. Of course it still hurts. That glue is only holding the cut closed, it's not a miracle drug."

She muttered something in Portuguese. "Well, it's too soon for more aspirin, but how about some more water?" She poked her head up and peered in the direction of the empty glass. Beside it was the digital clock. She bolted upright. "Oh, my God. Do you know what time it is?"

"Yup, three-thirty."

"But that means I slept for—were you awake the entire time?"

"Yup."

"Why didn't you wake me?"

"What for?"

"Mitch." She drew his name out into three syllables. "I'm supposed to be taking care of you."

"Okay, then want to know what I really want?"

"What?"

He patted the bed. "For you to lie here beside me again."

Accustomed to the darkness, he could see her head tilt to the side in doubt, and he could easily imagine the misgiving in her face. But she slowly slid back down and stretched out as stiff as a board.

He smiled to himself. "I wouldn't turn down a hug, either." Ignoring her sharp intake of breath, he urged her to lift her head enough for him to slip his arm beneath her neck.

She didn't resist, but instead, snuggled against him and sighed. "It's much easier not fighting."

He smiled and lightly kissed the top of her head. "No argument here."

A comfortable silence lapsed, and then she asked, "Do you think she'll call soon?"

"Around dawn would be my guess."

"Any particular reason?"

He tightened his arm around her, not threateningly but to soothe. "That's about the time Hope usually gets up."

"Oh." Her voice broke.

"Margaret will probably give her something to drink and eat and then make the call." He felt her feeble nod against his chest, and wished it weren't so dark that he couldn't see her face. Her body had already started tensing, her heart pounded against the side of his chest.

Too late, he realized he shouldn't have speculated on when to expect the call. It was going to be a hell of a long next three hours, and if the call didn't come, Terry would start panicking.

Damage control. That's what he needed. "Feel like doing me a favor?"

"What?"

"I'd do it myself if I could, but I'm not sure I'm up to it." The lie came out smoothly and without an ounce of guilt. This was more for her benefit than his.

"For goodness sakes, just tell me what you want."

"Eggs, toast, bacon. I'm starving. But if that's too much trouble…"

She sighed with exasperation and slid off the bed. "Of course it isn't. How do you want your eggs?"

Pancakes. They'd take longer to fix. "You wouldn't happen to know how to make banana-nut pancakes, would you?"

She frowned. "Don't those come ready-made and frozen?"

He smiled. "How about French toast?"

She looked somewhat relieved. "Sure. You still want eggs?"

"Over easy." He flipped on the lamp and started to lift himself from the bed.

She put her hands on her hips. "Stop right there. I don't need any help. In fact, I hate anyone else in the kitchen with me."

"I was going to the john. Do you mind?"

"Oh." She headed toward the door. "I'll bring your breakfast in here."

Mitch waited until he was sure she'd left the hall, and then went to his study and turned on his laptop, wishing like hell he knew what he was looking for. He'd already tried tracking Margaret's home address, to no avail.

When she'd applied for the nanny job, she'd requested a live-in position. After having struggled with the unfamiliar care of a small baby, Mitch had been tempted to accept the arrangement.

But something had stopped him. Some niggling little voice had cautioned him to go slowly. Not that he'd thought for one second that Margaret was a threat, but it was his privacy he'd been reluctant to give up.

Now he wondered if that little voice had been telling him more. Had he been so desperate for help that he'd chosen to ignore the warning?

He pushed the thought from his mind. It would serve no purpose to berate himself. Instead, he concentrated on the information coming up on the screen. No credit cards. No utility bills in Margaret Turner's name. The street address she gave him did exist, but the number didn't.

As soon as the agency that had referred Margaret opened this morning, he'd call and find out what information they had on her. It would be tricky to do and not raise suspicion, but he'd manage to wheedle something out of them.

He clicked out of one program and into another—official software that he'd confidentially gotten from one of his buddies at the Bureau. After retyping Margaret's phony address, he started the process of scrambling and unscrambling the information to see if she'd transposed numbers or played with the street spelling, or if there was any kind of relationship to the other information on her résumé.

He didn't know how long he'd been sitting there when he heard a soft noise behind him. He turned and met Terry's accusing eyes. A tray of food was in her hands. It kept lowering until he thought the plates would slide off.

Damn it. She was bound to get the wrong idea. "Terry…"

She took a deep breath, her breasts rising and falling with the intensity of it. "I guess it's time for me to start worrying."

CHAPTER NINE

TERRY WATCHED HIM EAT. She didn't touch a bite of the scrambled egg she'd made for herself. How could she trust him to tell her the truth? He'd lied. He'd reassured her there was nothing they could do but wait, and that Hope Katherine would be all right in the meantime. Words were cheap. Useless. She'd seen his face as he sat at his computer. She'd seen the frustration, the apprehension. Worse, she'd seen despair.

Who the hell did he think she was, anyway? Some fragile flower that would wilt under the pressure? What an arrogant simpleton. What a self-righteous jackass. What a—

"Why aren't you eating?" He lifted a strip of crisp bacon to her mouth.

She eyed his fingers. No, she wouldn't be so immature. "I'm not hungry."

He stared at her egg. "You were a few minutes ago."

"How can I trust you?"

"You think I poisoned your food? I wasn't even alone with it." He took a bite of the bacon she ignored. "Honey, I'm good, but not that good."

"Don't make jokes. I'm not in the mood."

The amusement fled his face, and he dropped the rest of the bacon on his plate. "Terry, I didn't do anything wrong."

"You lied to me."

"Not exactly."

How could he look her in the eyes and say that? She glared back. "You kept telling me not to worry, that all we could do was wait. Then I see you working in a frenzy as soon as I turn my back." She folded her arms across her chest. "You had no intention of telling me what you were doing. Or the outcome."

He sighed heavily. "Of course I would've told you. I'll tell you right now what I was doing."

"And I should believe what you tell me?"

"Look, Terry, I'm guilty only of shielding you from worrying about things that are out of our control. So, you want me shot at dawn, or what?"

The thought was tempting. "The only thing I want from you is—"

The shrill ring of the phone cut her off.

Her breath caught, her heart somersaulted. She reached the phone a second before Mitch, and managed a feeble "Hello."

"Ah, so you finally have the guts to talk to me." It was Meg, although her voice sounded odd, higher-pitched. Evil. "How are you, Teresa?"

Terry swallowed and closed her eyes against the light-headedness threatening to take her down. She couldn't panic. Not now. She opened her eyes and Mitch was in front of her, his hand on her arm, his gaze boring into hers, encouraging her to be strong.

"Meg..." She cleared her throat and realized she

had no idea what she was about to say. "How is Hope Katherine? Is she okay? Is she—please, don't—"

Mitch squeezed her arm and made a motion for her to stop. "Stay calm," he mouthed. "Don't feed her power trip."

On the other end of the line, Meg's piercing laughter rang in Terry's ears. It made her sick. "Teresa, did I hear pleading in your voice? Is the mighty Ms. Monteverde, queen of the society column, the social butterfly of Rio, actually begging *me* for something?" Meg cackled. "I'm so excited, I'm sitting here all atwitter."

Terry bit her lip. Mitch motioned to her about something but she didn't understand until he returned with a cordless extension phone. Slowly he pressed the button to listen in.

"Teresa, are you there?" Meg let loose a string of obscenities. "You bitch, you better not have hung up on me."

"I didn't. I'm here."

"Good thing for you. Where's Mitch?"

Terry's gaze had never left his, and he silently indicated not to tell Meg he was on the line. "He's right here."

"Ah, isn't that sweet? I'm sure he's given you one of his hunky shoulders to lean on. But then, you always did get the guys, didn't you, Teresa?"

Terry widened her eyes helplessly. What was she supposed to say to that?

"I'm talking to you, Teresa."

At Meg's sharp, edgy tone, Terry's breath caught. "Yes, I know. I—I just wasn't sure how to answer."

"What?" Meg screeched. "Have you so quickly forgotten Tom Samuels?"

Terry shook her head at the question in Mitch's eyes.

"He was a senior when we were sophomores. Chemistry lab?" When Terry didn't respond, Meg cursed. "How pathetic! The guy was head over heels for you and you can't even remember his name. I tried to console him. I even offered him my bed. But, no, he only had eyes for you, and you couldn't care less about him. Shall I name more?"

"Meg, I'm sorry if I—"

"Sorry hell. You're not sorry. You love the attention. Admit it."

Stunned, Terry stared helplessly at Mitch. He gave her a sign to play along. She swallowed the bitter taste of denial.

"Admit it!" Meg's breathing was heavy and uneven.

"Yes, I admit it."

"That's not enough. Explain what you're admitting."

"I love the attention."

"And?"

Terry briefly closed her eyes. She didn't want to look at Mitch. Did he believe what Meg was saying? Did he think Terry was a shallow, self-absorbed creature oblivious to the feelings of people around her?

"I'm waiting, Teresa." Meg's voice lowered dangerously. "It shouldn't be hard for you to remember the nasty things you did to me."

Terry gasped. "I befriended you. When you came to Rio, I offered you a job."

"A job...shit. Don't insult me." Meg paused, and all they could hear was her labored breathing. "Looks like you need more time to think about it."

"No, don't hang up. Please." Terry gripped the phone so hard her hand ached, and then she heard the click. "Oh, God..."

Meg's evil laughter startled her. "Fooled you, didn't I?"

More laughter. "Put Mitch on. I'm sick of talking to you."

"Meg, listen, let me talk a minute. I'm sorry I wasn't the friend you wanted. I didn't mean to—"

"I don't care what you say or mean anymore. Don't you get it? Now, put Mitch on or this time I will hang up."

Mitch had slipped an arm around Terry's shoulder. "She's sick," he whispered in her ear. "Don't let her get to you."

And then he gently pulled the phone out of Terry's limp hand.

"I'm here, Margaret," he said into the receiver, his concerned gaze still on Terry.

She turned away. She didn't deserve his concern or compassion or anything else. She was a horrible, superficial person who hadn't noticed the pain she'd caused.

"Yes, I understand," he said calmly, and Terry wished she'd picked up the other phone to hear what was happening.

"Let me get a piece of paper." He motioned for

Terry to bring him the small notebook next to the telephone book.

She looked over his shoulder as he wrote some street directions. He was so calm it both annoyed and soothed her. In big bold letters, he wrote, *one hour,* and then looked meaningfully at her.

"Okay, Margaret, we'll be there." He paused, his expression suddenly grim. "We won't be late."

"What did she say?" Terry asked the second he hung up.

"She wants us to go to a phone booth at the corner of McPerson and Lennon in an hour."

"At the end...what did she say at the end?"

Reluctance creased his face, and he stalled.

She stared him in the eyes. "What happened to being honest with me?"

Mitch scrubbed at his face. "She said if we wanted Hope to stay healthy, we'd better not be late."

"Oh, God." Terry sank onto a chair. "You said Meg wouldn't hurt her."

"It's a bluff. She wants to remind us she's in control."

"I saw your face. You didn't think it was a bluff."

His expression didn't waver. "She's talking about my daughter, for God's sake. Of course my knee-jerk reaction was to tense. But logically, I know what she's doing."

She stared at him, doing nothing to hide her distrust. "So what happens when we go to this phone booth?"

"She'll tell us when we get there."

"Are we supposed to bring anything? Money?"

"No, we wait for the call."

"But that doesn't make sense. Why can't she just tell us what she wants now? Why go to a phone booth?"

"How the hell do I know?" He sighed and rubbed his eyes. "Nothing she says or does makes sense," he said in a quieter tone. "She's calling the shots, and we have to be ready to jump through any hoop she holds out, period."

Terry rose and went to him. He hadn't slept all night, and he was still recovering from his head injury. "Come here," she said, taking his hand.

He narrowed his gaze, darting a suspicious look at the hand she'd wrapped around his. "What?"

"Come sit down."

"Why?"

She tugged him along. "Just sit."

He took the chair she'd vacated, and she moved around to the back and started massaging his neck and shoulders. Initially he tensed at her touch, and then he relaxed as she rubbed and kneaded.

"The phone booth isn't far from here." As she worked, she studied the paper he'd laid on the table. "Fifteen minutes away, would you say?"

"About that. And about ten minutes away from that dive she sent us to yesterday."

"So that means she probably isn't that far away, right?"

"That's my guess, unless of course, that's what she wants us to believe. But I doubt it. She hasn't been here that long and she knows this area. Besides, she doesn't think we'd look for her."

"Why not? That's what you do. I mean, that's part of your job."

"She knows all we want is Hope back, and she's keeping us on a short leash, filling up our time with fools' errands. It's been barely twelve hours."

Twelve hours? Terry shook her head in denial. It couldn't be only twelve hours. She looked at the clock over the door. He was right, but so much had happened....

Mitch grunted and angled his shoulder away from her. "Take it easy, champ."

Her gaze flew to the area she'd been kneading and immediately jerked her hands back. "Sorry."

He reached behind and brought one hand back to his shoulder. "It feels good, Terry. Just ease up on the right side. I got nicked by the bat."

"You didn't tell me about that."

"It's just a bruise."

She pushed his shirt aside. It was bruised all right—a rainbow of blue, purple and scarlet. Enough to make her stomach turn. "Ah, Mitch..."

"It's no big deal. We need to leave here in half an hour. Will you be ready?"

"I'm ready now."

"Leaving in half an hour will already get us there early."

When he rotated his neck, she gently rubbed the muscles around the base. She wondered why he didn't ask her to stay behind while he went to get the phone call. Not that she would agree but he had asked the first time. Did it have to do with Meg's instructions?

Or did he have a private reason? Like not wanting to leave her alone.

She looked down at him, the way his strong, capable hands were clasped on the table, the wide breadth of his shoulders, which had readily assumed the responsibility of their daughter, the way he remained calm and in control. Everything about him seemed so familiar to her, and yet it had only been twelve hours since they reunited.

In some ways, she knew he had to hate her, yet he still tried to shield her. He was an honorable man. He'd protect the mother of his child whether she deserved it or not.

"I think I'll take a quick shower," she said, withdrawing her hands and dragging her palms down the front of her skirt. "Need me to do anything first?"

He shook his head, turned and looked at her. "Use my bathroom."

"The guest bathroom is fine. You'll probably want to—"

"Use mine."

She frowned, but then she got it. There were too many reminders of Hope Katherine in the other bathroom. Again, he was trying to protect Terry. She swallowed, nodded and hurried to find the suitcase he'd brought her.

God, but she was a wreck…exhausted…worried… emotional. She could barely carry a thought to its rational end. Yet Mitch was injured and hadn't had any sleep at all. How could he hold up much longer? This was all so unfair to him, caught in the middle of her mess. A mess she'd slowly started creating a long time ago.

Meg was right about some of her accusations. Terry had been self-absorbed, or at least engrossed in a rebellion against her father. She'd been in reaction mode, instead of making conscious decisions. If it rankled her father, Terry was in for a pound.

And now Mitch was caught up in the chaos of her own making. He didn't deserve any of it. And God help her, Terry didn't deserve him. But she could make things right for everyone.

THEY MADE THE DRIVE in virtual silence, which was fine with Mitch, except he couldn't shake the feeling Terry was up to something. Either she'd given herself one hell of a talking to while in the shower, or there was something she wasn't telling him. She was calm. Too calm. Like a woman who'd made a big decision and no longer felt the weight of uncertainty.

"Nervous?" He glanced over at her. She had her hair tied back in a short ponytail, and she wore jeans and a plain white cotton shirt.

She smiled. Not a great smile but it was there. "No."

"I am."

She blinked at him, concern flickering suddenly. "Did Meg call back while I was in the shower?"

"No." He turned his eyes to the road. "But I suspect we're about to hear what she wants."

"No reason to be nervous. We pretty much know what that is." Her voice was calm again, and he didn't miss the irony of their role reversal.

It made him smile a little. "Let's agree on who talks to her."

"Sure. I will."

That made him lose the smile and he turned abruptly to her. "I think I should."

She shook her head. "I totally disagree. She was letting us wait until I got on the phone. So what if I inflamed her. At least it got her to act."

"Yeah, but we want to make sure she acts as rationally as possible."

She gave him a bland look. "Meg? Rational?"

"You know what I mean. Look, I think that's the phone booth." He mumbled a curse. "Someone's using it."

"Take it easy. We're early."

Mitch steered the car to the curb and parked near the corner, then turned to stare at Terry. "All right. What's going on?"

She widened her eyes. "What do you mean?"

"What did you do, take a Valium?"

She reared her head back and frowned at him.

"If you did, that's fine. I just wanna know why you're suddenly so relaxed."

"Like you said, we need to remain levelheaded."

He didn't buy it. Or maybe it was just him. Hell, he was tired and edgy and ready to punch a wall. His judgment wasn't exactly sound right now. "Look, the guy's leaving the booth. Let's get it before someone else decides they want to reach out and touch someone."

She got out quickly, beat him to the booth and slipped inside.

"I thought we agreed I'd talk to her." He slipped his keys into his jeans' pocket and then joined her in the booth.

"What are you doing?" Clearly startled, she backed into the corner. "There's not enough room for both of us."

Her fresh rose scent surrounded him, coated his skin, calmed his nerves, infused him with new vitality. "I'll do the talking."

"Mitch, please don't fight me on this. I know what I'm doing."

Fear blocked his air passage. He stared down at her determined face, the flash of fire in her eyes, and he knew they were headed for trouble. "Talk to me, Terry."

"There's nothing to talk about. We don't even know what she wants yet."

That was the thing. They did know. Margaret wanted Terry. He grabbed her wrist to get her attention. "If we don't stick together on this, we don't stand a chance."

Uncertainty flickered in her eyes. "I would never jeopardize Hope Katherine's safety."

"Not knowingly."

She twisted her wrist around, trying to free herself. He loosened his grip but didn't let go. She grunted with one more unsuccessful try, then shot him a dirty look. "What makes you the authority? I know Meg better than you do."

"Not according to her," he said, and saw his stinging words hit their mark. "She thinks you ignored her."

Terry's face paled and her lower lip quivered.

"I didn't say that to hurt you. I doubt it's even true, but that's Margaret's perception, and that's what we're dealing with."

This time when she tried to jerk out of his hold, he let her go. But before she could turn away, he ran his thumb across her cheek.

"Don't."

"Come on. I know the woman's delusional." He held her chin so she couldn't look away. She lowered her lashes to shutter her eyes. But he didn't have to see them to know he'd wounded her. "We start bickering like this and she wins."

"What if she was right about me?" Terry slowly opened her eyes and the pain he saw there put an ache in his heart.

He started to refute her when the phone rang. They both made a move for it. He grabbed it by a hair.

"Mitch," he said into the receiver.

"What's the matter?" It was Margaret, sounding tired and stressed. "She's too chicken to talk to me?"

"We're both here," he said, holding the phone so Terry could hear.

"In the booth together? How cozy. You both make me want to puke."

Anger brought color to Terry's cheeks. When her mouth parted, he shook his head and covered the mouthpiece.

Margaret swore, and then went into a coughing fit. "Are you two listening to me?"

"We're listening." Mitch held Terry's gaze. Margaret didn't sound good at all. He hoped she wasn't too sick to take care of Hope.

"I'm going to tell you what I want, and I'm only going to tell you once. Got it?"

"Got it," he confirmed. "But first you have to do something for us."

"I don't have to do anything for you."

"We have to know that Hope is all right."

"We went through that, you idiot. She can't talk."

"Put her near the phone."

There was silence and then heavy wheezing that made him and Terry exchange worried frowns. The phone dropped on the other end, making a horrible cracking sound, as though it hit a concrete floor.

He covered the mouthpiece again. "Does Margaret have asthma or some respiratory problem?"

"I don't think so. She never missed work. But she sounds awful."

He heard her pick up the phone and he quickly took his hand away from the receiver.

"I've got her," Margaret said. "What do you want me to do, make her cry?"

"No," Terry and he shouted together.

Margaret laughed until it turned into a cough. "I wouldn't do that to Hope. I'm insulted you think I would."

He shook his head at Terry. The woman was a lunatic. "Margaret, here's what I want you to do—"

She cut him off with a shriek in their ears. "You don't tell me what to do. Don't you two morons get it yet? I hold all the cards." She stopped to take two labored breaths. "I tell you what *I* want."

"Which is?" Mitch lowered his voice in an effort to calm her.

"A hundred thousand dollars in small bills."

He kept looking at Terry as the silence stretched, not allowing himself to hope "Is that it?"

"Yeah, right. You're the idiot, not me." Margaret mumbled something unintelligible to herself. "The diamonds. I want the damn diamonds. Teresa, do you hear me?"

Mitch stared hard at Terry. There was no denial in her face, no confusion—only anger.

"Which diamonds, Meg?" she asked coolly, wrapping her hand around Mitch's and guiding the phone closer to her mouth.

"You know damn well what I'm talking about. Hayes's diamonds, the ones you took with you from your safe."

Terry's laugh was short, harsh. "You did set me up. I didn't want to believe it, but—you really hate me that much."

"You do have the diamonds. A million bucks worth?"

"Yes, I have them."

If she hadn't covered his hand, Mitch would have dropped the phone. She'd lied to him. He'd outright asked her if there was any reason she'd still be followed, and she'd lied.

Talk about being naive. She obviously wasn't the helpless victim she'd have him believe. This was about diamonds and money. Margaret was right. He was an idiot. He'd actually begun hoping there was a future for him and Terry. But when this was over, so were they.

CHAPTER TEN

TERRY'S MIND RACED with replays of the past couple of years, odd bits and pieces about Meg that now fit together. She pushed the maddening thoughts aside. She had to concentrate on the present...on getting Hope back.

"Okay," she said calmly, eyeing Mitch, who didn't look calm at all. He seemed angry. "It's going to take me a few hours to raise the money." She glanced at her watch. Nina could help her but the time difference was a problem. "Maybe not even until tomorrow." She paused, took a deep breath. "In the meantime, I have to see Hope Katherine."

"Oh, you'll see her all right." Meg's laugh was pure evil. "You didn't let me finish. I have one last demand." She paused long enough for dread to slither up Terry's spine, for Mitch's jaw to tighten. "I want you, Ms. High-and-Mighty Monteverde. I want you to bring the money and the diamonds. Alone."

Terry breathed deeply. "And then you'll give me my baby."

Meg started laughing again. "Your baby?"

Terry's head grew light. "Meg, please—"

"Please what? I think you're finally starting to realize how capable I am—of anything." Meg coughed, her breathing strained when she added, "Tell you what…I'll give you some more time to think about it."

"No, don't hang up. I'll do anything you want. I'll go to you now while Nina raises the cash. *Anything* you want me to do I'll—"

Before Terry knew what was happening, Mitch wrenched the phone away from her. "Margaret, we're not doing a damn thing until we know Hope is all right. Is she near the phone?"

Terry's anger ebbed at his interference when she realized Hope Katherine should have reacted to Meg's shrieking and coughing. Yet Terry hadn't heard a peep. She brought a fist to her mouth, fear clawing at her insides, and she pressed against Mitch to be able to hear.

Meg swore and mumbled something about Mitch butting in. "Wait a minute. She's crawled over to the radiator."

"Radiator!" Mitch paled, "She could get burned."

"Shut up. I'm not stupid. The damn thing hasn't worked in years." The phone dropped, making that awful crashing noise again.

Terry drew back and stared accusingly at Mitch. "You had no right to grab the phone away."

"And you had no right to promise her anything."

"It's me she wants. We already know that. I have every right to offer myself." When his expression remained implacable, she added, "Wouldn't you do the same?"

"That's different."

"Bull."

His nostrils flared and he started to respond, but abruptly turned his attention back to the phone. "Is she there?"

Terry pressed closer again to hear. Mitch angled the phone toward her.

"I got her." Meg's voice softened. "She sure is getting big. Heavy, too."

Terry bit her lip, torn between gratitude that Meg had a soft spot for Hope Katherine, and the agony of not being able to hold her own baby, of feeling the child's weight in her arms.

"Okay," Mitch said. "Under her left arm she has a ticklish spot. Poke her gently and she'll start to giggle."

Terry stared at Mitch, an onslaught of mixed emotions filling her. She envied how well he knew their daughter, how much they'd bonded, while she had missed so much of Hope Katherine's young life.

Within seconds Terry heard the giddy burst of gurgling laughter. Her heart swelled with happiness at the sound, and her eyes instantly teared up with relief.

She moved her mouth closer to the receiver. "Hope Katherine?"

Another giggle, and then silence. Had she recognized Terry's voice? Did she remember her mother at all?

"Satisfied?" Meg started coughing again, and Terry prayed Hope Katherine was out of range. When the sputtering stopped, Meg added, "You have five hours to get the money and diamonds."

"We'll get everything, but five hours might not—"

Terry was cut off by a severing click.

"Damn her!" She struggled for a breath. "Damn her."

Mitch replaced the receiver, and then took her cold hand in his. "Come on. Let's go."

She allowed him to lead her out of the booth, her mind in such a daze she followed him to the car without a word. Once she'd gotten inside and he'd climbed behind the wheel, her panicked thoughts swirled into a whirlpool of fear and anger.

"We've got to hurry." Her gaze flew to the dashboard clock. "Nina will be at work by now. She can get us cash."

"Terry, you've got to calm down."

"But it isn't much time." She rubbed the sudden chill from her arms. "Nina can do it. She'll find a way."

"Terry…"

"If there is a problem, at least she can have the diamonds while we wait. And me."

"Terry!"

She jumped at his harsh tone and looked at him.

"You need to—"

"What? Calm down? Go to hell." She wrapped her arms around herself. "Did you hear Meg? She's sick. We've got to get Hope Katherine back before something happens."

"I agree, but we aren't going to accomplish that by going off half-cocked."

She stared at him in disbelief. "We know what Meg wants. We give it to her. Simple."

"What? You think you're going to march into her trap—" A horn's blare warned him that they'd started

to cross the center line and he jerked the wheel, right-
ing them just in time. He cursed, took a deep breath.
"You're not exchanging yourself for Hope."

"Are you insane? Of course I am."

"The hell you are." He didn't even look at her.
He kept his gaze straight ahead, the anger and tension
radiating from him as thick as smog. "We'll give
Margaret the money and the—" he paused, shook his
head "—diamonds. She's sick. She won't want to
hang around and argue. She may even realize she's
too ill to take care of Hope. I'll be the one to meet
with her."

"You can't do this. You can't take over. We agreed
we're in this together."

"Sweetheart, we agreed on a lot of things." Anger
darkened his eyes when he sent her a resentful look.
"Didn't we?"

"What are you talking about?"

"When were you planning to tell me about the diamonds? Or were you?"

She frowned. "I started to…yesterday, but we were
interrupted. Besides, what's the point?"

"The point?" He snorted with disgust. "I asked
you if there was anything I should know about why
someone would follow you."

At a genuine loss, she waved an agitated hand, and
then smoothed her hair. "With Hayes dead, I didn't
think it mattered. In fact, I truly didn't give the diamonds much thought at all. It wasn't as though I was
keeping them for myself. I—"

She stopped herself short. It was better he didn't
know.

They came to a stoplight, and he turned to give her a piercing stare full of distrust, and worse, disappointment. "Where are they?"

She pressed her lips together. Exactly what she didn't want him to know. He'd try to stop her from meeting with Meg, and once he had the diamonds in his possession, Terry would have only the cash to offer Meg...assuming she could get it in time.

After a long tense silence, he asked, "Are you going to tell me?"

Terry wanted to curl up into a ball and hide. Mitch's demeanor had changed since the call. He blamed her for everything that had happened, no matter what he claimed to the contrary. Maybe it was about the diamonds. Maybe he thought she was going to take them and make a run for it.

God, she didn't want him to believe that of her. If he only knew... She could explain, but then he'd get to the diamonds before she could.

She cleared her throat and swallowed hard around the lump lodged there like a granite boulder. "No, I'm not."

His sharp intake of breath told her he hadn't expected that answer, and when he looked at her with such vast disappointment, she nearly coughed up the truth. Instead, she looked away.

"Why?" He pulled the car into his driveway and let it idle while he angled toward her. "If you had no intention of using them for personal gain, why not tell me?"

"Because you'll interfere with me turning them over to Meg."

"Right."

"That's the truth."

"That's garbage. You know damn well I have no problem turning them over to her if it'll get Hope back."

She finally understood, the idea making her queasy. "But you don't trust me to do it because you think I'll make a run." Her voice cracked. "And leave my daughter?"

He sighed, leaned his head back and passed a hand over his face. "Of course I don't. I figure you didn't expect to be called on the diamonds. That you'd get Hope back and the two of you would ride off into the sunset with a cool million."

"You are so wrong." She couldn't believe she thought they might actually be a family. He was wrong. But so was she. About him.

"Then tell me where the diamonds are."

She opened the car door. He grabbed her wrist to stop her.

"Mitch, I have to call Nina."

"You're going to blow this, Terry. You're going to walk right into Margaret's trap. You know damn well what she has in mind for you."

"Do I have a choice?"

"You can trust me."

She laughed and jerked away. "Especially since you've been so forthright thus far.

"You're as guilty as I am in that regard, but we sure as hell had better start working together now if we want you and Hope to both make it out of this alive."

Terry gasped, oxygen fleeing her lungs. "You said Meg wouldn't harm her. You said she regarded Hope Katherine as her own child by now."

"I know what I said. But Margaret is physically sick. No telling how that's affecting her stress level, or her judgment."

"You bastard!"

He stared at her, anger and fear darkening his face. "Go ahead, blame me. Hope that makes you feel better."

"You think I'm some..." She trailed off, shaking her head as she got out of the car. It wasn't worth it. She needed to call Nina. Getting the ransom together was all that mattered.

She started up the walk to the front door when she remembered she didn't have a key. The garage door started to creak open and she ducked beneath it and hurried to the unlocked kitchen door.

After she got the phone and rang Nina, she went to the kitchen window and peeked through the blinds. Mitch still sat in the car in the middle of the driveway. She couldn't see his face, but the slump of his shoulders was unmistakable.

Nina answered after the third ring and Terry explained briefly and semicoherently what she needed. Her sister assured her that raising the money would be no problem and that she'd call back within two hours with the details of the wire transfer.

Terry hung up, forcing herself to breathe deeply, reciting over and over in her mind that Hope Katherine was going to be just fine. She heard a car door and looked out the window. Mitch had left the car in the drive and was approaching the garage. She dabbed at a stray tear before he came through the door.

"You talk to Nina?" Lines of exhaustion creased his face and the normally vivid blue of his eyes was dull and lifeless.

She nodded. "She doesn't think there'll be any problem. I should hear from her in a couple of hours."

"Okay, that gives me some time," he muttered half to himself, his gaze wandering off.

She didn't like the way he said that, the way he suddenly seemed oblivious of her presence. "Time for what?"

His gaze drew back to her, cautious, reluctant. "Look, I don't want you to get your hopes up, but I may know where Margaret is hiding out."

"What?" Her pulse sped up. "How?"

"It's a hunch, okay, so don't get too excited."

"A hunch?" Hysterical laughter threatened. "We don't have time to explore a hunch. We'll do exactly as Meg asked, period."

He shook his head. "It's more than a hunch—while she was talking, did you hear background noise?"

Terry shook her head, afraid to hope he knew what he was talking about.

"Trucks, large semis. They make a distinct sound when they're coming to a stop. In the space of that short phone call, I heard at least four of them."

She frowned and shrugged. "So there's a stop sign outside Meg's apartment."

"They didn't just stop or I would have heard them accelerate again. Those trucks were parking."

"That still could be anywhere."

"Yeah, except for the location of the bar and phone booth Margaret used. I doubt she would have gone too far to leave the note or get the pay phone number."

In spite of herself, hope started to build. "And you know of a truck stop in that area?"

He nodded. "Several."

Hope crashed. "Several? What good does that do us? We only have a few hours. We can't check every possibility."

"You're right. Time is a premium." He reached into the small cupboard over the refrigerator and brought down a metal box. "That's why I need your promise to stay put and wait for the call while I go investigate."

She watched him unlock the box with a small key he'd withdrawn from his pocket. "Of course I'll wait for the call."

He looked up and waited for their gazes to meet. "Not just for the call, you have to promise to wait for me."

"What else would I do?"

One side of his mouth lifted in caustic amusement. "I can't imagine."

"Sarcasm won't help."

"You're right." He flipped open the safe box and withdrew a gun. "I apologize."

She couldn't drag her gaze away from the ugly, cold piece of metal. "What's that for?"

"Insurance," he said as he stuck the gun into the back waist of his pants under his jacket.

"I don't like it."

"Neither do I, but it's a good thing I know how to use it." His face was a cold mask, his eyes shards of blue steel.

This was the other side of Mitch, the one devoid of emotion, wired for action, determined to get results, damn the means. It was a side that frightened her. But it was also this part of the man that would get their daughter back.

"Will you call me?"

"Will you be here?"

She nodded. "Of course."

"No heroics, got it?"

She stiffened. "You don't care what happens to me."

He didn't deny it, only stared hard at her for another minute, his expression impersonal, before leaving through the garage door.

Terry sank onto a kitchen chair, crossed her arms on the table, and rested her forehead on them. She wouldn't cry. That would gain nothing. Besides, it was too late for tears.

MITCH GOT ON the freeway and figured he had about two hours left to locate Margaret. That is, if it took Terry's sister the entire two hours to get the money and call Terry. After that, Terry would still have to get to the wire office and get the diamonds... wherever the hell she had them stashed.

He doubted they'd been among the things he'd collected for her at the apartment. Number one, he saw nothing that would have concealed them, and anyway, she probably wouldn't have sent him in the first place if the gems had been there.

It still galled him that she'd lied about taking the diamonds. Lied by omission, anyway. But as he'd had a chance to calm down, his suspicion that she'd planned on running with the contraband subsided as well.

If she'd been looking for personal gain, she wouldn't have been living in that dump. She'd had plenty of time to fence the diamonds if all she wanted was the money. But she'd been a single mother, on the run, and if all she wanted was a secure future for her daughter, who could begrudge her that wish?

Was he being a sap again? Was it just so damn hard for him to believe that Terry was capable of pure, disgusting greed? Did he have no good judgment whatsoever when it came to her?

He truly didn't think so. For one thing, he had to respect and admire the fact that she was willing to exchange herself for Hope. That was no bluff either. She'd do it, and that's why he had to hurry and get to Margaret before she called again. No telling what Terry would let the woman talk her into doing if it meant she'd get to see Hope.

No matter what else he thought of her, Terry was proving to be a good mother, and he sure as hell didn't want to see anything happen to her. Margaret was out for blood. That was one thing of which he was certain.

Fortunately, he had more than a hunch as to where she was hiding.

CHAPTER ELEVEN

HAVING TO WAIT might as well have been a death sentence handed to Terry.

She scrubbed the kitchen floor, wiped down the cabinets, and then she tackled the living room and bathrooms, even though everything was virtually spotless.

She'd gone into the nursery about an hour ago but quickly realized she couldn't handle being there. Hope Katherine's fresh baby smell lingered in the brightly colored clown sheets, the Disney mobile that hung over her crib and the army of stuffed animals that lay scattered about.

Much as she didn't understand Mitch's ability to emotionally detach, she recognized the importance of keeping a clear head and trying to stay as objective as possible.

If sitting and staring at Hope Katherine's toys had brought only misery, Terry probably would have welcomed it. God knew she deserved the torture, but being among her baby's things drove every rational thought out of her head. And that she couldn't afford.

She dropped the sponge and cleaner into the kitchen sink and glanced at the wall clock. Nina would be calling within the next half hour, and Terry prayed she'd have good news. If for some reason her sister was unable to raise the money, Terry had another plan.

After peeling off the rubber gloves and dropping them into the sink as well, she patted her jeans pocket. She knew the diamonds were there in a small red velvet pouch, but somehow, feeling the stones, proving she had the means to set Hope Katherine free gave her enormous comfort.

Mitch was wrong about Meg. If they could just meet face-to-face, Terry was certain she could reason with the woman. Yes, she was sick, both physically and mentally, but Terry had known her for over ten years. They had shared some laughs once, girlish gossip about the campus hunks.

Later, even their professional relationship had had some moments of camaraderie, some feminine bonding. Not much, admittedly. Terry had been too busy taking the company to the next level of excellence. But surely they'd be able to connect again. Meg already had a soft spot for Hope Katherine. Terry would just have to capitalize on that, appeal to Meg's maternal instinct and convince her Hope Katherine would be better off with Mitch.

Terry shuddered at the thought of what possibly lay in store for her. But she was hopeful she'd talk Meg out of any more violence. She'd offer to get Meg help, provide medical attention and not press charges, anything to get her safely institutionalized.

Except the woman was crazy—maybe too crazy.

Terry snatched up the sponge and started scrubbing the sink again. She couldn't start second-guessing herself. Appealing to Meg was her only hope. Glancing at the phone, she prayed Nina would hurry and call. If Mitch returned home first, the plan would end up in smoke.

HE DIDN'T TRUST HER. Mitch punched speed dial on his cell phone. Not that he had anything to report to Terry, but he wanted to make sure she was still at his place. He was reasonably sure she hadn't left, mostly because she needed to wait for the calls from Nina and Margaret, but he was cutting it close.

So far he'd eliminated one of the two places he figured Margaret might be hiding. If he was wrong about the second, God help him....

"Terry?"

The phone on the other end had been picked up, but no one said anything.

Icy fear threatened his air passage. Had they been set up? "Terry?"

"Yeah." She was out of breath.

"What's wrong?"

"Nothing." She paused, her breathing labored. "I had to run for the phone."

"Are you alone?"

"Of course." Silence. "Is something wrong? Have you found her?"

"No." He rubbed his jaw and sighed. Behind him, someone leaned on their horn. The light had turned green and he proceeded through the intersection. "When you didn't answer right away, I thought maybe..." He shook his head, weary, his imagination obviously in overdrive. ''Never mind. You heard from Nina yet?''

''No.''

He didn't like the way she'd hesitated. Or was that his imagination again? ''Did you try calling her back?''

''Um, no, I didn't think it would do any good. Nina will call as soon as she has something. Besides, I didn't want to tie up the line.''

''Right.'' Something in her voice wasn't kosher.

''Oh, you had a call. From Lily Garrett Bishop. She says you have her number.''

''Yeah, thanks.'' She was probably calling about the search for his father. He'd been wishy-washy, wanting Finders Keepers to look for the man one minute, and calling off the search the next. Dean Harding, a former detective the agency used, had taken on the job, but Mitch had put him on hold till the situation with Terry was resolved. In the meantime, Dylan and Lily were keeping the file open. It would be decision time again soon. After they got Hope back.

''Okay, well, I've got to go.''

Unease crawled up Mitch's spine. ''Go where?''

She hesitated. ''I meant I want to get off the line.'' The slight hesitation was just long enough to make the hair on the back of his neck stand.

''Of course. I'll call later.'' She hung up before saying goodbye.

He came to a stop at a red light and stared at the dashboard clock. She'd had to run for the phone? What was that about? Knowing Terry, she would have practically been sitting on top of it waiting for

Nina's call. Unless she'd already received it. And Margaret's call, had that come already?

He cursed and started punching in Lily's phone number. She wasn't in the office so he tried her cell. She answered on the first ring.

"Lily, it's Mitch."

"Hey, I've been trying to reach you. I've got more good news."

He closed his eyes, rubbed them with the heel of his hand. "My father?"

"Yeah, you all right?"

"Look, I can't talk about him right now, but I need a favor."

"Shoot."

"Terry Monteverde is at my place. I need someone to watch her."

Static disrupted the line and he couldn't hear her response. While he waited for it to pass, his thoughts strayed to his father. Immediately Mitch put the mental brakes on. He couldn't handle thinking about a reunion now. Damn it, he still wasn't sure he wanted one.

"Mitch?"

"I'm here."

"You said you needed me to watch Terry? As in keeping her under surveillance?" Lily's tone was guarded. No telling what she thought this was about.

"I can't explain now, but yeah, that's about the size of it."

"You want this done now?"

"For about an hour." He heard her unspoken hesitation. This wasn't something she'd normally do. "Can you just trust me on this, Lily?"

"Yeah, I trust you." She paused, and he could hear her soft sigh. "Mitch, when I tell you what I found out about your father, you're going to have to trust me, too."

TERRY WAS OUT the front door before the cab turned into the driveway. Luckily she hadn't waited for it on the street or she would have missed Mitch's call. She had to slow down, think clearly. Mistakes weren't an option.

She got in and gave the cab driver the address where she could pick up the money Nina had wired, and then sat back, closed her eyes and reviewed Meg's instructions. Terry was to go to the corner where they'd used the phone booth earlier. Meg would pick her up there and take her to Hope Katherine. Obviously it wouldn't be that simple, but at least Terry would have a chance to talk with Meg.

What else could she have done but respond? Everything had happened so quickly, Terry hadn't had time to form Plan B. God help her, she hoped she wouldn't need it.

Yet a nagging little voice echoed like a warning in her head. Meg was crazy all right, but she was sharp enough to figure out that calling early would mean getting Terry alone. It had been pretty damn obvious she hadn't intended for Mitch to be in on the exchange. If there really would be an exchange… money and diamonds for Hope Katherine. Or was Mitch right? Was Terry walking into a trap?

She couldn't think about that right now. If she kept focused on Hope Katherine, she could handle this. The thought of holding her baby again brought such a lump to her throat and tightness to her chest that she had to roll down the window and take several deep breaths.

When she sat back, the driver's dark eyes appeared in the rearview mirror. "You okay, lady?"

She forced a smile. "I'm fine."

He grunted something she didn't understand, and then he went back to watching the road. Several times they made eye contact again, but he said nothing.

Minutes later they pulled up to the curb of the money wiring office. The cabbie agreed to wait while she ran inside, and she felt the weight of his stare until she disappeared through the door.

A hundred thousand dollars was a lot of money, especially broken down in small bills, and coming to this type of office made it obvious she was picking up. When she carried the tote of cash outside, she was aware of the cabbie's gaze glued to it, and hoped like hell she was just being paranoid. Not that she had much choice. Only fifteen minutes left to meet Meg.

She gave him the cross streets to the phone booth and tried to concentrate on the route he was taking, which seemed right from what she remembered. Occasionally, he looked at her in the rearview mirror, but he didn't seem threatening, but almost concerned, which of course he couldn't be.

Gripping the handles to the tote tighter, she went from staring at her watch to shooting impatient glances at the growing traffic.

"You sure you gave me the right cross streets?" the driver asked suddenly, startling her and making her jump.

"I'm sure."

"There ain't nothing around there but a seedy bar. No place a girl like you wants to be going."

She swallowed. There was an odd kindness in the older man's voice. "Look, I want you to do something for me. I'll pay you a hundred dollars on top of the meter amount."

He frowned into the mirror. "What?"

"A woman is picking me up. I want you to follow us without her knowing." She grabbed a fifty-dollar bill out of her purse. "Here's half the money now, and you get the other half later."

"Later when?"

"After you follow us, leave the meter running and wait outside for me."

"How long are you gonna be?"

"I'm not sure. I hope only about ten or fifteen minutes."

His eyes narrowed. "You ain't doing nothing illegal, are you?"

"No." She held his gaze. "I swear to you I'm not."

"Well, okay. I just don't want to miss out on any rush hour traffic. Especially those airport runs. They pay good."

"I promise to make it worth your while. But it's important that I have your word you'll wait."

"Sure, lady, no problem."

She handed him the fifty just as they pulled up to the phone booth.

"What about what's on the meter?"

"You want me to settle it now or when—" Terry shook her head, her heart starting to pound. She'd pay him now. There was a chance he'd never see her again. No one would. "Here. This should take care of it."

To her horror, her hand shook so hard she could hardly pass him the bills. He noticed, and raised his suspicious gaze to her face.

"Lady, is there something you should be telling me?"

"Terry," she said, and then cleared her throat when her voice came out creaky. Maybe he'd wait for her if he saw her as a person and not just another fare. "My name is Terry."

"Nice name." He grinned, displaying a gleaming gold tooth.

"Thank you. It's short for Teresa." She glanced outside. No sign of Meg yet.

"Oh, yeah? That's my daughter's name. The second oldest one. God bless me, I have five. All daughters." He rubbed his graying beard. "Only two bathrooms. That don't give me no time to shave."

Terry laughed softly. This man wouldn't leave her now.

She straightened when a white Buick stopped behind them. She saw Meg right away and opened the car door. "Okay, there's my ride. Remember..."

He waved her away. "I remember."

She tried unsuccessfully to still her quivering hands

as she got out and closed the cab door. Meg was busy looking around as Terry approached the passenger side of the Buick, probably making sure no one had followed.

Terry's gaze flew to the empty back seat. Where was Hope Katherine?

"What the hell you waiting for, an engraved invitation?"

Meg's tone was brittle, her eyes red-rimmed and wild as she leaned over and opened the passenger door. It made Terry shiver. "Get in before I change my mind and leave you here."

Terry moved quickly, seating herself, and tucking the tote between her knees. "Where's Hope Katherine?"

Meg gave her an oddly amused look before putting the car into gear. "Hope Katherine? Where did you come up with that?"

"Katherine is what I named her when she was born."

Meg shook her head. "It still boggles my mind to think of you as a mother. It must have been a rude awakening for a selfish bitch like you to find out you were pregnant."

She stiffened at the insult but said nothing. And then she saw the cab pull away from the curb, enter the intersection and turn left. Her heart sank. So much for her judgment of people.

"You listening to me?" Meg cursed, and shook her frizzy head. "Of course not. You never listened to me. You never had the time of day for me."

"That's not true—"

"Shut up!"

"Where's Hope Katherine?"

"I told you to shut up." She'd pulled out into the street, but she suddenly looked confused, as if she wasn't sure which way to go.

Oh, God.

Terry closed her eyes against the rising panic in her chest, the nausea churning in her belly. Hope Katherine had to be all right. She had to be. Terry opened her eyes again to find Meg watching her.

"Feeling out of control stinks, doesn't it?" Meg laughed and steered the car to the right.

"Please, Meg, I'm begging you, just tell me we're going to see my baby."

"*Your* baby?" Anger flashed so fiercely that Meg's hands jerked and the car swerved and missed a telephone pole by inches. "See what you made me do?"

She righted the car as Terry sat silently, helpless to say anything that wouldn't provoke the woman.

"Your baby, hell. What kind of mother leaves her kid on a doorstep? You didn't even get the right doorstep, damn it." Spittle had dried and caked around her mouth. She looked as though she hadn't washed her face or combed her hair in days. "No, Hope isn't your baby anymore. You're too pathetic to be a mother."

"Meg, you know what kind of trouble I was in. I had no choice but to leave her with Mitch."

"Mitch." She spat the name as she turned the car down a narrow alley. "I was willing to give everything to that man, but he's no better than you. I was good enough to be the nanny but that was it. You're two of a kind.''

She parked the car near a four-story building that looked as if it might have been a warehouse at one time. But now half the windows had been shattered and obscene graffiti covered the battered walls.

Not a soul was in sight, nor was there evidence that anyone had been around recently. Even the labels of the broken Miller bottles and discarded Twinkie wrappers littering the gutter were faded as if left some time ago.

Terry let out a long slow breath. ''Is Hope Katherine in there?''

''Get your butt out of the car and see for yourself.'' Meg climbed out and looked around before heading for the door—or what used to be the door. The hinges were rusted out and the metal sheeting hung loosely. Anyone could walk in. Amazing that the place hadn't been condemned.

Terry got out and followed, anxious that Meg hadn't mentioned the money or diamonds. She hadn't even glanced at the tote bag. Which to Terry's thinking meant Mitch was right. For Meg, this was about getting even with her.

''We have to use the stairs,'' Meg said over her shoulder, and then swore when her voice was drowned out by a loud swishing sound.

''What was that?''

''Goddamn trucks.'' Meg sent a vicious glare in the direction of the freeway. ''They make so much damn noise you can't hear yourself think.''

Excitement simmered in Terry's veins. Maybe

Mitch was right. Maybe he did know where they were. "What trucks?"

"On the other side of the building there's a kind of rest stop they—" Meg stopped short. "Don't get any ideas. They're too far away for you to go running for help."

"Why would I do that? I came here voluntarily. With the money and diamonds. I expect you to hold up your part of the bargain."

Meg had just stepped across the threshold but she turned suddenly, and before Terry could back up, grabbed a hold of her hair. She gave a savage yank that made Terry shriek in surprise and pain.

"Don't go getting all high and mighty on me, you stupid bitch." Meg twisted her hand around, tightening her hold on Terry's hair and bringing her face so close she could see the madness growing in the woman's eyes. "I don't have to listen to you anymore. *You* listen to *me*."

Tears sprang to Terry's eyes, and she swallowed hard, forcing back the pain and fear. "Of course."

A sadistic smile lifted the corners of Meg's mouth. She gave a final yank, staring into Terry's eyes with purpose and pure hatred, and then released the tangle of hair. "Come on. Hope's been left alone long enough."

Terry pressed her lips together and meekly followed Meg toward the stairs. Once she got a glimpse of Hope Katherine, she felt reasonably sure she could take Meg. The woman was thinner and seemed frailer than she'd been in Rio. Of course Meg had insanity on her side, pumping fresh adrenaline, discounting the cost of her actions.

The stairs were as unsafe as the rest of the building and the thought of Hope Katherine being carted up and down them made Terry queasy. Just knowing her baby was inside this hellhole sickened her. She pushed the thought aside and forced herself to focus on what she had to do. Meg was unpredictable, which meant Terry had to be twice as alert.

Thankfully, Meg stopped on the second level and led the way into a large open area. Her breathing was labored after the short climb and she'd started to cough.

Terry exhaled slowly. As soon as she saw Hope Katherine…

"I hated bringing her here," Meg said suddenly, a trace of regret in her voice. "But I didn't have a lot of choice. I honestly hadn't expected Mitch to find you so soon."

The spark of humanity gave Terry hope. "I'm sure you've taken good care of her," she said as she furtively searched the room for Hope Katherine. "Mitch assured me you've been terrific with her."

"He said that?" Meg arched her brows. "I'm surprised he even noticed."

"Oh, he did. When I saw your résumé and realized who you were, he told me it wasn't possible, that you'd been an excellent nanny. That I had to be mistaken about the name."

"Hmm…" She began a violent coughing fit, and Terry was alarmed to see blood on the tissue she brought away from her mouth.

She laid a hand on Meg's arm. "Are you okay?"

Meg jerked away. "Don't pretend you care about me. Too late for that."

"But you're obviously sick and need to see a doctor. I don't care about the money or the diamonds. Take them. Get to a hospital. I won't look for you. Neither will Mitch." Out of the corner of her eye, Terry saw movement near the window and her pulse leaped.

A rattle jingled.

"Hope Katherine?" She moved in that direction, her knees suddenly so weak she thought she might collapse. And then she heard the soft coo, a gurgle. "Katherine?"

"Yeah, go ahead. Go see if she recognizes you."

Even Meg's hateful sneer didn't faze Terry. She dropped the tote and ran to where Hope Katherine was strapped into a car seat. Her cheeks were rounder, pinker, and her hair seemed darker. She smiled when she saw Terry.

Tears came hot and fast to Terry's eyes as she stooped to unbuckle her baby. "Mama is here, sweetheart." She kissed her smooth baby cheek, anxious to feel her small warm body in her arms again. "Mama is going to take care of you."

"The hell she is."

That's all Terry heard before thunder struck her head, and everything went black.

CHAPTER TWELVE

"BARNES." Mitch answered his cell phone, knowing in his gut this was going to be a bad call.

"I don't think she's there," Lily said without preamble.

He exhaled sharply. "You got there soon after we talked?"

"About a half hour."

"Let me try calling and I'll get back to you. She's probably sticking close to the phone."

Lily was surely curious as hell, but to her credit, she didn't ask what this was about. "Okay, but I even tried ringing the doorbell. I was going to pretend I was stopping by to see you."

"She didn't answer?" Mitch swore to himself. What the hell was he going to do now? "Okay, thanks."

"Mitch, wait."

"Yeah?"

"Whatever it is, let me help."

He stared at the red light, watched it turn to green. But he didn't move until someone behind blasted their horn at him. "I'm not sure you can."

"There's got to be something I can do."

He thought for a moment. If he was right and Terry

was going to meet Margaret at the abandoned Parker Building, he just might need someone to take care of Hope once he interrupted the party. If he was really lucky, Terry hadn't gotten there yet.

"You know the Parker Building near the freeway?" he finally said, and when Lily replied she did, he added, "Meet me there as soon as possible and I'll explain everything."

"I'm on my way." She clicked off, and Mitch knew he could count on both her immediate help and discretion.

Not that he had much choice. Damn, he wouldn't have guessed Nina could get the money wired that fast. Or that Margaret would have called back so soon. Unless she figured moving quickly would keep Mitch out of the picture.

He suppressed the urge to hit the steering wheel. He had to get a hold of himself. Anger or fear would only get someone killed. He swallowed back the panic and desperation at the thought of anything happening to Hope. Or Terry. In spite of everything, he still had feelings for her.

He made it past the intersection without killing himself or anyone else, and then turned down the narrow alley. It had been a while since Mitch had prayed, and he hoped God hadn't given up on him, because he was praying like hell now, almost willing there to be a car in the abandoned parking lot.

As soon as he got past the alley he saw the white Buick. A few hundred yards off to the left was a cab with a driver sitting behind the wheel and staring at the sagging Parker Building.

Had the man brought Terry here?

Optimism seeded and grew inside him, and it was all he could do not to floor the accelerator. Trying to avoid making noise, he cruised closer to the cab. The driver seemed torn between keeping an eye on him and watching the building. Once he pulled alongside the man he lowered his window.

"Hey, you waiting for a fare?" Mitch asked casually, but there was no mistaking the man's guarded expression.

"In this neighborhood?"

Mitch looked pointedly at the building. "Why else would you be here?"

"What are you, a cop? None of your business." The man's bushy dark brows drew together in scowl, and he started rolling up his window.

He hated to do it, but Mitch pulled out his FBI badge and held it out his window for the guy to see.

The man paled and immediately rolled his window back down. "I don't want no trouble."

"Did you bring a woman here? Early thirties, dark hair, about five-four, pretty..."

The man muttered something in a language Mitch didn't understand and spread his hands. "She swore she was doing nothing illegal."

Mitch's heart started to race. "How long ago?"

"The other woman, she picked her up and I followed." He shrugged his shoulders. "Maybe ten... fifteen minutes ago. But I have nothing to do with her illegal business."

"Why did you follow?"

"The young pretty woman...Terry...she says she

will pay me to wait for her. I have to earn a living, that's why I wait. I don't know her or her illegal business." He waved an agitated hand toward the building. "Can I go now?"

"How did you know her name?"

"She told me. After I picked her up." He made the sign of the cross, and then kissed his pursed fingertips. "I swear by all that is holy I did not know that woman before today. She seemed nice. I thought she might be in trouble."

Mitch sucked in a breath. She was in trouble all right. "The other woman, how was she acting?"

He circled his index finger near his temple. "Crazy. I have to go now."

"They entered the front entrance?"

The man nodded. "I think they went to the second floor. I could see something move, maybe shadows. But there has been nothing for several minutes now."

"I need you to stick around." Mitch didn't bother finding a parking spot. He turned the car off and got out. The conversation had taken only seconds. It felt like an hour.

"But I have done nothing." The cabbie lifted his hands, palms up. "This is America. There is no reason to keep me here."

Mitch snorted. He'd heard that one before. But of course, this was different. Everything was different about this case. He silently cursed himself. That was the thing—this wasn't a case. This was personal. Hope and Terry were inside, and he better not pull his lone wolf routine. He could live to regret it.

"Look, you're not in trouble. The woman…Terry…

she isn't involved in anything illegal. You're right, she's the one in trouble and I may need your help.''

''What can I do? There is nothing—''

''What's your name?''

Reluctant, he frowned. ''Chez.''

''Listen, Chez, all you have to do is sit here like you've been doing and wait for another lady to come. Her name is Lily. I want you to tell her what you've told me and I'll pay you twice what's on your meter. And I'll triple whatever Terry promised you.''

Chez's confused gaze followed Mitch's hand as he went for the .22 tucked in his waistband. At the sight of the gun, the man's eyes widened.

He met Mitch's eyes. ''Why would you pay me? You are not here officially?''

''Not exactly.''

Chez started to roll up his window. ''I don't want to get involved.''

Mitch stuck his hand in the way and winced when the glass made hard contact with his wrist. ''There's a baby up there…Terry's daughter. The crazy woman took her. We're trying to get the baby back.''

Chez froze. Slowly, cautiously, he rolled down the window. ''Mother of God, why are the police not here?''

Mitch shook his head, rubbed his wrist, while he held the man's gaze. ''No police yet or someone could get hurt.''

Chez exhaled loudly and scratched his beard. ''Go. I'll wait for this Lily.''

''Tell her Margaret has Hope inside. I don't know

if she has a weapon. But if you or Lily hear more than two shots fired, call the police. If I come to the window and wave, that means Lily should come and get Hope. Otherwise, tell her not to come inside. No matter what. You got all that?''

Chez gave a solemn nod. ''I got it.''

Mitch put a hand on his shoulder. ''Thanks.''

Chez made the sign of the cross again, and just as Mitch took off for the entrance, he heard the man say, ''May God be with you.''

Mitch choked back a lump of emotion. Screw himself. God had better concentrate on Hope and Terry.

''WAKE UP, damn it, I didn't hit you that hard.''

Terry blinked and tried to focus. The walls wouldn't stop moving. Up and down, in slow motion, like a distorted carousel. She closed her eyes again, afraid she'd get sick or pass out.

''Oh, I forgot what a damn wimp you are.'' Meg's shrill voice rang in her ears. ''Stay awake.''

Ice-cold water hit Terry's face. Gasping, she tried to squirm away, but something restricted her movement. Her arms...she couldn't move them. Her legs...

She squinted at the crudely tied rag binding her ankles together. Behind, her wrists felt like they were manacled together with barbed wire.

''Get that stupid look off your face.'' Meg stood in front of her, legs slightly apart, her right fist clenching a chipped blue mug. ''Do I need to get more cold water?''

''No. I'm awake.'' Terry struggled to sit up but she couldn't seem to straighten from her slouched position. The swimming in her head made her feel as if she'd been drugged. "Where's Hope Katherine?"

Meg laughed until she doubled over into a coughing fit. After regaining control, she straightened and wiped her runny nose with the back of her sleeve. The look she gave Terry was one of pure hatred. "Where do you think she is? Watching you. Watching how pathetic you really are."

Terry's frantic gaze scanned the room. It horrified her to think her baby had to witness any of this. But she saw no sign of Hope Katherine. Her gaze went back to Meg. Had the woman finally tumbled over the edge?

"Over there. Against the wall." Meg jerked her head with impatience in that direction.

Terry twisted around to see, and then sighed with gratitude that Hope Katherine was busy playing with a Raggedy Ann doll.

"She likes that toy. I bought it for her." Meg's expression had softened as she watched the baby.

"I can tell she does. That was nice of you, Meg."

The hatred returned to her face when Meg turned back to Terry. "Don't think I don't know what you're doing. Being nice to me now doesn't count. I needed you as a friend in college. I adored you, Teresa. You wore the right clothes, said the right things, hung out with all the cool people. I thought you were the most perfect woman I'd ever met. And the only time you paid attention to me was when you needed tutoring in math."

Terry shook her head. "That's not true. I invited

you to a couple of parties but you were so shy that—"

"You never invited me to anything."

"What about the winter ball after-party my sorority had? Remember? I'd asked you to come but you were busy."

Meg frowned as though she were trying to remember. Terry herself had forgotten until Meg brought up the math tutoring. She'd refused to accept payment so Terry had invited her to the party as a thank-you. The entire sorority had pitched a fit because they thought Meg was weird, but Terry had insisted.

"The winter ball...junior year..." Meg's voice trailed off as if she were lost in the past. Her frown deepened, and then she slowly turned that wild-eyed glare on Terry. "You stupid bitch. I didn't go."

"Yes, but I did invite you."

"Not your party." Frustration radiated from her as she started to pace the room. "I didn't go to the winter ball so how could I go to your after-party?"

"I'm sorry, I didn't know."

"Of course you didn't. You had all the dates you wanted. No one asked me."

"You didn't need a date. You could have—"

"Shut up!" Meg covered her ears. "Don't try to confuse me."

Terry held her breath while Meg resumed her pacing, hoping the woman would expend some of her pent-up energy and rage. She twisted around to get a look at Hope Katherine again, whose wide dark eyes were following Meg's movements.

Her pink daisy outfit was clean, and so were her

face and hands. She looked healthy and happy enough, although Meg's sudden outbursts of temper and shrieking voice must be affecting her in some adverse manner.

Meg's mutterings had stopped and Terry turned back to find the woman watching her with so much malice it made her flinch.

She swallowed. "I brought your money, Meg, just like you asked. I don't know why you have me tied up."

She didn't mention the diamonds that were still in her pocket. Meg hadn't found them yet and Terry figured she might need them as leverage.

But Meg didn't seem concerned with them. At least not yet. "You don't know why I tied you up." Meg's thin lips turned up in a spine-tingling smile. "Like you wouldn't have tried to take me down if I hadn't."

"No." Terry offered her denial as skillfully as possible. "I simply expected you to live up to your part of the bargain."

"My part?" Meg laughed, coughed, swore. "This is my show. It's all my part."

"Please, Meg, if you care for Hope Katherine at all—"

"I told you to shut up!" Meg drew back her hand and lunged forward.

Terry pressed her lips together, waiting for the blow.

A creaking noise coming from somewhere near the stairs stopped Meg cold. She spun toward the sound, her body tense and her hands fisting. "Who's there?"

No response.

Terry didn't see anything. Much as she wished someone would march to her rescue, she figured it was a cat, or the wind catching one of the loose doors or iron shutters.

Meg stood perfectly still and stared in the direction of the stairs. Even when Hope Katherine's gurgling broke the silence, she didn't turn around. She stayed focused on the landing as if she expected someone to suddenly materialize.

Capitalizing on Meg's preoccupation, Terry twisted her wrists against the tight binding and winced when the abrasive cord dug into her skin. She gritted her teeth and tried again. The pain was great, and the attempt in vain. She sniffed, swallowed, and tried again.

From behind the rusting radiator, Mitch held his breath. Damn it! He hadn't meant to alert Margaret. But when she drew back, ready to strike Terry, anger made him stupid.

With so many shattered windows, the place was drafty, and he remained still, hoping Margaret would blame the wind. He didn't want to make a move yet. She had a gun, a small caliber judging by the size. He recognized the slight bulge under her sweater at her waist—the same place he carried his gun. He wondered if Terry had seen it, or was aware Margaret had it.

For that matter, why hadn't Margaret pulled it out when she'd heard the rock he'd kicked hit the wall?

"What are you doing?" Margaret ran to Terry and yanked her hair, while Mitch used the opportunity to get in a position to see what was happening. "You're not going to get loose so quit trying. You're only making me mad.''

"The cord's too tight. I'm losing circulation in my hands.''

Margaret chortled. ''You have a lot more to worry about than that.''

Terry's eyes widened slightly, but she lifted her chin. ''Meg, you have to let us go. You know Mitch won't stand for anything less.''

''Mitch can't think straight right now. Not enough blood going to his brain. It's all ended up in his third leg.'' Margaret laughed. ''Get it?''

Terry frowned.

Margaret shrieked with disgust. ''Ever since he started looking for you, you're all he's thought about. Used to make me sick listening to him on the phone asking about you. After, he'd stay in his study, moping, staring at the walls.'' She went to the window and stared at the freeway. ''I'd cook his favorite dinners, make sure his laundry was done, run errands for him, wear clothes I couldn't afford, and he never gave me a second look.''

''Men are dense sometimes,'' Terry said in a teasing voice, but Mitch could see she was still trying to work herself free. ''Did you tell him you were interested?''

Margaret turned away from the window and fixed Terry with a murderous glare. ''Like that would do any good. You're the only one he wants.''

A sad smile touched the corners of Terry's mouth. ''You're wrong. The only reason he wanted to find me was to hold me accountable for leaving Hope Katherine.''

"That's not true. Don't try to trick me."

"It's true, all right." Her laugh was bitter, ironic. "I wish it weren't, but it's true."

Mitch clenched his jaw. He couldn't afford an emotional response to that humbling admission. He had to keep his focus on rushing Margaret without anyone getting harmed.

Obviously, even Margaret heard the wistful sincerity in Terry's voice. A strange look crossed her face. "You're wrong," she said, her misgiving clear. "He wants you."

Terry sadly shook her head. "Mitch doesn't want to get too close to anyone."

He clenched his jaw tighter. Where the hell did she get that? Or maybe this was a ploy to distract Margaret. Still, Terry looked awfully convincing...and convinced.

Margaret lowered herself to a crouched position in front of Terry, looking doubtful yet intrigued. "You really think that, don't you?"

Terry's eyes were glassy. "I know it. We had a great night together, an evening of mystery and secrets and forbidden passion. It was also temporary. No commitment. A one-night fling. That's what made it appealing to Mitch."

Mitch did all he could to hold his tongue. She'd never given him a chance to talk about the future. Obviously she'd forgotten that she was the one who'd left the bed before dawn without a stinking word.

Margaret lowered herself to the floor and sat cross-legged in front of Terry as if they were two old friends having an amicable chat. "He loves Hope."

"I know he does." Terry sagged against the wall, her shoulders drooping. "That's why I left her with him. I knew no one would take better care of her. But accepting responsibility for his child and actually cultivating a relationship are two different things."

Margaret sat silently for a moment, a thoughtful frown creasing her face. "I've known him for almost a month." She lifted her smug chin and cackled. "Longer than you when you come right down to it."

Terry made a noncommittal movement with her shoulder.

"I think you're wrong about him," Margaret said, starting to tense again. "You didn't have to watch him mooning over you, wasting all those nights. Hell, I practically offered him my body and he didn't give me a second look."

"Don't take it personally." Terry rested her head against the wall and briefly closed her eyes. "I'm learning not to. He doesn't know how to be anything but a loner. He can't even compromise on Hope Katherine's name."

"What are you talking about?"

"I named her Katherine. He named her Hope. In concession I've been calling her Hope Katherine. Not once has he referred to her that way. She's Hope. That's it."

Mitch seethed with denial and anger. Keeping his mouth shut and staying detached was the most difficult thing he'd ever done. The only upside was that Margaret seemed to be mellowing. Maybe being treated as Terry's peer and confidante was all she needed to be subdued.

"You may be right about some of it." Looking confused, Margaret shook her head. "If I were to let you go right now, would you go back to him? Or would you take Hope and run?"

Terry blinked, wariness straightening her posture. "I'm not sure."

His heart dropped to his stomach. She hadn't even hesitated. Damn her. She had no intention of sticking around. She just couldn't admit it.

Margaret started shaking her head and mumbling. He couldn't hear what she said, but it wasn't anything good judging by the look on Terry's face.

"Meg, can you untie me? I swear my hands are going numb."

"And I should care?" Margaret stood abruptly. "Don't think this little heart-to-heart changed anything."

"So what—" Terry stopped, cleared her throat. "What do you intend to do with me?"

"I don't know yet." Margaret held her head with both hands. "Just shut up! I'm trying to think. So just—"

She started wheezing, and then coughed with such violence she clutched her stomach.

Mitch flexed his right leg, making sure it wasn't asleep, and then bolted for Margaret. He was halfway across the room before she spun around and saw him. With surprising speed, she grabbed the gun from her waistband. Before she could level the weapon on him, he tackled her to the floor.

She hit the concrete with a thud and groaned, but kept hold of the gun. Mitch tried to kick it out of her hand. She pulled away in time and started screeching like a banshee as she swung around to take aim at him.

Terry screamed.

Hope started to cry.

Mitch pointed his gun and pulled the trigger.

CHAPTER THIRTEEN

THE GUN FLEW out of Meg's hand. She hit the ground screaming and cussing. A crimson stain spread across her sleeve as blood oozed out of her upper arm.

"Don't move, Margaret." Mitch kicked her gun farther away. "I don't want to have to hurt you."

"Hurt me? You stupid bastard, you just shot me." Meg wailed, clutching her shoulder and wiggling to sit up.

"Don't move around. You'll be okay as soon as I get a tourniquet around that arm."

"Don't let me die, Teresa." Meg's eyes were large and terrified. "Don't let him—" She erupted into another coughing fit.

Terry took a calming breath. "He's right, Meg. Don't move around so much, and I'm sure you'll be fine." She looked up at Mitch and gestured with a tilt of her head. "Hope Katherine is over there."

He gave Terry a brief glance, loathing in his eyes, before he headed for their crying daughter.

His expression was so blatantly hostile it took her aback. She watched him pick Hope Katherine up, heard his sigh of relief as he held her close. He whispered something as he gently stroked her back and she immediately stopped crying.

Meg stopped coughing and sobbed. "I think I'm dying."

Mitch took another long look at Hope Katherine, ran a finger down her chubby cheek as though assuring himself she was really there and okay. And then he set her back in the car seat and knelt in front of Meg. He tore off a strip of the discarded rag Meg had used to bind Terry's ankle.

Fear chilled Terry to the bone. Something was wrong. Really wrong. Was he angry because she'd come without him? "Mitch, cut me loose and I'll tend to Meg."

He gave her that same awful look again, one that made her skin crawl and her heart pound, and for a moment she thought he might ignore her.

"Mitch!" The dark-haired woman from yesterday—Lily—came running from the stairs. "You okay?"

Behind her was the cabbie whom Terry had asked to wait. But she'd seen him drive off. She blinked. The threat of tears already blurred her vision. He was still there, walking toward her, smiling nervously, his gold tooth gleaming.

She half laughed, half sobbed.

"Yeah, everyone's fine." Mitch stared down at Meg when she let out a shriek of protest. "Even you. Not that you deserve to be."

The cabbie stepped gingerly around Meg, his eyes narrowed in curious fear at her curled up on the cold, hard floor, and then he headed straight for Terry.

"Lily, you mind tending to her," Mitch said, indicating Meg with a thrust of his chin. "I'm taking Hope to the hospital."

"Is something wrong with her?"

"Nothing appears to be, but I'd rather err on the side of caution."

"Good idea." Lily's confused gaze went to Terry and then she nodded at Mitch. "I'll stop the flow and then call the police and the paramedics."

The cabbie made the sign of the cross as he stooped to look at Terry. "You almost gave me a heart attack. You okay?"

She nodded, trying like hell not to cry buckets. "I saw you leave."

"I circled the block so she wouldn't know I was following you." He fiddled with the binding around her ankles. It was knotted too tightly for him to free it.

Terry's gaze strayed to Mitch. He had lifted Hope Katherine to his chest and whispered to her while he grabbed a hold of the car seat. He didn't give Terry a single glance.

"I thought you'd left me. Thank you." She forced a smile for the cabbie and blinked back more threatening tears. "What's your name?"

"Chez." He stood and looked around the mostly bare floor. "I need a knife or something sharp to free you."

Meg's sudden yelp drew their attention.

Lily sighed and tied off the dirty tourniquet. "Shut up. You'll live."

Mitch carried Hope Katherine toward Terry and she straightened in anticipation, anxious for a closer look at her baby. She gasped when he kept walking past her.

Even Chez and Lily gave him odd looks.

He stopped near the landing and turned around. "Oh, and would someone untie her?" Without looking at Terry, he indicated her with a jerk of his head, then headed down the stairs with a wide-eyed Hope Katherine.

TERRY RUBBED her sore, but thankfully free wrists as she watched the police and paramedics escort Meg to the ambulance. The crimson stain on the concrete floor made her feel physically ill and she had to turn away from the sight of it.

Lily startled her by coming up behind and then taking one of Terry's hands to inspect the red welts left by the cord. "Nasty-looking stuff. Didn't the paramedic give you anything to put on this?"

At the look of compassion Lily gave her as their eyes met, Terry's throat burned with a build up of emotion. "I don't need anything," she said softly. "Do you know which hospital Mitch took Hope Katherine to?"

"I think I can guess." Lily hadn't let go of her hand. "What the hell is wrong with him, anyway?"

Terry shrugged and lowered her gaze. "He's probably angry that I met Meg without him."

"Well, sure, I can understand that, but still, he's acting like a jackass."

Terry looked up, surprised his friend would speak of him that way.

Lily's attention stayed on Terry's wrists. "Don't

get me wrong. I like Mitch. He's a great guy. But I recently had a baby and if anyone had done—'' She visibly shuddered. "Let's just say I can guess how you're feeling about now."

Terry sighed. "Thanks, I, um..." Her voice cracked, and Lily looked up with a kind smile. She tried again. "That wasn't Mitch. You know he's not like that...." Terry shrugged. "I think maybe he heard me say something to Meg that upset him. But to tell you the truth, I don't even remember everything I said to her."

"Of course you don't. You were in shock, I'm sure." A considering frown drew Lily's eyebrows together. "Overhearing something would explain his attitude. The cab driver thought Mitch was your husband. He said Mitch looked ill when he heard you were in here with Margaret."

Terry straightened. "Where is Chez?"

"He had to go. He said he wouldn't be surprised if he saw you again."

At the thought of the man's kindness and bravery, a tear escaped and slid down Terry's cheek. She quickly dabbed it away.

"I know," Lily said, slipping a comforting arm around her shoulder as she guided them toward the stairs. "You can let it all out on our way."

"Where are we going?"

"To the hospital so you can have that bump on your head looked at."

Terry stopped. "I don't need to go to a hospital."

"Are you sure?" Lily asked with a secret smile.

It took Terry a minute to get it, and she smiled

back. Lily Garrett Bishop had just become a friend
for life.

MITCH DRAINED his third cup of stale black coffee
and paced the lobby for the second time. No way
would he have let that doctor throw him out of the
examining room if it hadn't been for Hope. She kept
crying, wanting to go to Mitch and squirming so
much the doc couldn't do his job.

The sight of her in his mind's eye, lying in the car
seat on the bare floor, surrounded by all that filth and
decay, made his gut roll. It had been so damn tempting to aim for something other than Margaret's arm.

An unbidden image of Terry flashed in his mind,
sitting against the wall in a crumpled heap, her wrists
and ankles helplessly bound. He crushed the empty
foam cup and slammed it into a wastebasket. God,
but he'd been a fool about her.

"I need to talk to you."

At Lily's voice, he turned around. His gaze immediately went past her to Terry, standing near the
reception desk. "What's she doing here?"

"Getting checked out."

"She looked okay to me."

"Margaret clobbered her over the head. She's got
a lump the size of Texas near her crown." Lily met
him toe-to-toe. "What the hell is wrong with you?"

He stared dumbly. "My daughter was kidnapped.
What the hell do you think?"

"Excuse me, but isn't she Terry's daughter, too?"

He turned toward the vending machine for another
cup of stale coffee.

Lily got in his face before he could put a coin in the slot. "Mitch Barnes, this isn't like you. What gives?"

"Stay out of this."

She arched her brows. "Who called who asking for help?"

"It's not that I don't appreciate your—"

"Knock it off." She folded her arms across her chest and stepped aside. "Get me a cup of that junk, will you?"

"Sure." He dug for more coins in his pocket. "But I gotta warn you, the stuff sucks."

Her grumpy expression stayed put, and she mumbled, "That's not all that sucks."

He ignored the comment and got them each a cup of black coffee. "Obviously you haven't given the police a statement yet."

She accepted the coffee and shook her head. "I gave them a brief summation. Terry helped me fill in the holes. Bill Swanson was one of the detectives who responded, and he said we could go down to the station after we finished up here."

"Good thing you know half the force." He sipped the bitter brew, aware that Lily was staring intently at him.

She wasn't going to give up hounding him. Tenacity was part of what made her so good at her job. It was just one of the many reasons he liked her. But damn it, she was going to have to stay out of this one. She was taking Terry's part without knowing all the facts.

Terry had used him...pure and simple. Now that it

looked as though she was off the hot seat with the Brazilian officials, and Margaret and Hayes were no longer threats, Terry was free as a bird. She could go back to her nice, cushy life in Rio, take Hope with her and never give him another thought again.

God, he was such a fool.

"Tell you what—" Lily dumped her coffee in the trash "—after they release Hope, I'll take her back to your place and stay with her until you and Terry finish giving your statements."

"Thanks, but I don't want her separated from me. She's been through enough already."

"You think she'd be happier at the police station? Come on, Mitch, she knows me, and she'll be glad to be back in familiar surroundings."

She was probably right. But that meant he'd have to be alone with Terry. "I could take her home and you could take Terry to the police station."

Lily gave him a wry look. "You fired the shot that brought Margaret down. Call me crazy, but I bet the police just might want to talk to you."

Her sarcasm needled his pride. "There's a lot you don't understand, Lily."

"Apparently, because you aren't acting like yourself."

"Mr. Barnes?"

The nurse's voice drove all other thoughts but Hope from his mind, and he turned, encouraged by the woman's warm smile.

"Your daughter is doing just fine. The doctor said she's free to go now."

"Thank you." He sighed with relief. "Thank you very much."

When the nurse turned to leave, Mitch started to follow her. Lily touched his arm. "Why don't you find out about Terry, too?"

Tempted to tell her he didn't give a damn how Terry was doing, he kept his mouth shut. Besides, that claim would be a lie. He did care, which really galled him.

"Cut her a break, cowboy." Lily gave him a small shove. "It's just as hard being a mother as it is a father."

He hesitated another moment before heading down the white sterile hall, reminded of the days after he'd hurt his Achilles tendon. Surgeries, shots and rehab. Having to depend on someone to bring his food or help him to the bathroom. That nightmare had been his life for a while.

Now he was living a new nightmare.

What the hell was he going to do? Terry didn't want him, and his feelings for her were such a jumble right now, he didn't know what he wanted. But they had a child, which meant neither of them would walk away unscathed.

He got to the room where he'd left Hope with the doctor and nurse. The door was slightly ajar and he pushed it open farther and peeked inside.

Terry sat on the bed, holding Hope in her arms.

Every nerve in his body went on alert. His first impulse was to snatch Hope from her. He took a deep breath instead, and slowly entered the room. The young doctor stood off to the side, reading a chart.

He looked up when he heard Mitch. "Mr. Barnes, did you see the nurse? Both your daughter and wife are doing fine."

Mitch's and Terry's eyes met. Neither said anything.

"I think the little one is hungry." The doctor smoothed Hope's dark hair. "Other than that she's in excellent condition.

"You," he said to Terry, "are going to be fine if you take it easy. That was a nasty bump." He turned back to Mitch. "You'll have to keep an eye on her for the next twenty-four hours. Her brain cells took quite a beating. You may have noticed some disorientation, but it should have passed by now. If she still has problems thinking clearly, we'll do a brain scan."

"Can we leave now?"

At Mitch's abruptness, the doctor frowned. "Sure," he said, and stepped back to give Mitch room.

He reached for Hope, but Terry looked reluctant to give her up. "I'd better carry her. You might get dizzy."

Terry moistened her lips, the hurt in her eyes undeniable as she nodded and held Hope out to him. She touched the baby's cheek one last desperate time before he brought her to his chest.

The doctor held out a hand for Terry as she swung her legs off the hospital bed. "Okay?"

She nodded and gave him a small smile.

"I'll leave you then." The doctor nodded at Mitch, disapproval in his expression. "Call if there are any problems."

So everyone thought he was the bad guy here.

Tough. He said nothing until the doctor left the room, then he glanced at Terry. She was pale and her hair was a mess. "We have to go to the police station. Lily will watch Hope."

"Do we have to go now?" She reached a hand out to touch Hope, as if reassuring herself her child was actually there. "We just got her back."

"Yup." He started walking out of the room.

"Have you found out how Meg is doing?"

"Why would you care?"

"She's sick, Mitch. She wasn't in her right mind."

"You're awfully forgiving. She took your baby daughter, remember?"

"I remember a lot of things," Terry said softly as she tried to keep pace with his longer stride.

"Yeah, well, so do I." Guilt forced him to slow down. That and the way her lower lip quivered.

"Can we stop at the desk and check her progress before we go to the police station?"

"Do what you want." He headed for Lily without looking back to see if Terry had stopped or was behind him.

"Everybody okay, I trust." Lily smiled at Hope and gave her a light poke in the belly. Hope gurgled, but she was too cranky to giggle.

"Yeah, except Hope's hungry."

Lily took the baby. "You're hungry, huh? Well, I think we can do something about that." Hope began to fuss but Lily quickly calmed her down. "What's Terry doing?"

Mitch glanced back. "Checking on Margaret."

"I asked. She's already out of surgery. I think

they're more concerned with the respiratory infection she has.''

Was he the only sane person here? ''You asked about her?''

''Of course.'' She patted Hope's back. ''The woman is obviously mentally ill.''

''Right.'' He rubbed the back of his neck, so damn tired suddenly he could hit the floor and crash for two hours. ''You'd better get going with Hope.''

''Terry's coming. We can all walk out together.''

He said nothing when Terry went straight for Hope and Lily. She teased Hope's hand until the baby wrapped her tiny fingers around Terry's thumb.

Terry's eyes glistened but she laughed softly and they walked all the way to Lily's car like that.

''She looks so big,'' Terry said as soon as they parted company with Hope and Lily. She climbed into the passenger seat of his Explorer while he got behind the wheel. ''How tall was she the last time you took her to the doctor?''

''I don't remember.''

''Really?''

He ignored the slightly sarcastic tone and kept his gaze straight ahead. But he knew she watched him. He felt every ounce of her stare. He even sensed when she finally looked away, although she didn't say another word the entire trip to the station.

He was tempted to look over at her, make sure she was all right. From his own experience, he knew a blow to the head was nothing to take lightly. The thought that they'd both gotten clobbered in the past twenty-four hours caused an unexpected tug at his lips.

"What did she hit you with?" he asked, and when Terry didn't answer, he glanced over at her.

Her eyes were full of wary curiosity as she stared back. "I don't know. It happened so fast."

"Did you need stitches?"

"No."

"Will you be able to talk to the police?"

"Why wouldn't I?"

He swung his gaze back to the road and rubbed the side of his neck. Tension had formed a monumental knot. "The doctor said you might be disoriented."

"I'm fine."

"You remember everything that happened?"

"Yes." She shuddered and folded her arms across her chest. "I think so."

He eyed her suddenly defensive posture. "What?"

"Why are you asking me these questions? I feel like I'm being interrogated."

Mitch stiffened. What was he doing? Trying to rationalize the things she'd said about him?

"Look, Mitch, I'm sorry I didn't do things your way. And I'm sorry I got myself in a mess you had to fix. I only wanted to do what I thought was best for everyone. But I screwed up. Haven't you ever screwed up before?"

"Oh, yeah." He looked purposefully at her. "I've screwed up."

Hurt darkened her eyes, and she looked away. "What do you think will happen to Meg?"

"She'll get what she deserves."

"Mitch, stop it. You're not a cruel man."

They stopped at a red light and he turned his attention solely on her. "Don't sound so pious. What you feel is guilt, not sympathy."

"What?" She looked at him as if he were something she'd found on the bottom of her shoe. "Oh, that's right, I almost forgot. You're above human emotions. You wouldn't recognize sympathy and compassion if it slapped you across the face."

He stared at her a long silent minute. "Is that what you believe?"

She wilted against the car seat. "I don't know what I believe anymore."

For the five minutes it took to get to the police station, he said nothing. But as they turned into the visitor's parking he said, "By the way, you'd better be thinking about where you'd like me to drop you off when this is over."

CHAPTER FOURTEEN

GIVING THEIR STATEMENTS went routinely and quickly, along with the expected chastisement for not calling the authorities as soon as they knew Hope had been taken. Terry gave a brief outline of what they suspected was Margaret's involvement in the embezzlement and smuggling charges made against herself. At times she seemed a little vague and distracted, but Mitch knew it had to do with the head injury and the trauma of the past few hours. Anything important they left out could be added later.

Hell, he was distracted, too.

Good thing Lily knew Bill Swanson, as well as the other detective involved in the case. Mitch knew them, too, though only through Lily.

However, he knew them well enough to feel like an idiot. Listening to Terry recount the past few hours, watching her struggle to maintain her composure had him acting like a rookie agent. He butted in when he knew better and made excuses when he should have been factual and objective. At one point, the other detective suggested Mitch go get a cup of coffee. That really annoyed the hell out of him.

That both detectives seemed rather taken with her didn't help his sour mood. It made him see red. Made him wonder what kind of spell she'd cast over him. One minute he couldn't wait to get rid of her, the next he wanted her in his arms. But that wasn't going to happen.

"I guess that about wraps things up." Bill Swanson smiled at Terry. "If you folks remember anything else, be sure to give us a call."

Mitch grunted his acknowledgment. He'd been so preoccupied he hadn't realized the interview was over.

"Of course, Detective. Thank you." Terry started to stand but looked a little unsteady. Swanson quickly left the corner of the cluttered desk where he'd been sitting and helped her to her feet.

"You sure you shouldn't be staying the night in the hospital?" he asked, putting an arm around her shoulders.

"No, that's unnecessary. I need to get home to my baby." Her anxious gaze darted to Mitch. He looked away.

Swanson didn't miss the exchange. "Before you go, let me make sure I have your correct address and phone number."

"It's the same as mine," Mitch said, and out of the corner of his eye, saw Terry tense. "Anything else?"

Swanson half smiled. "Nope. You can go."

"We know the way out." Mitch gestured for Terry to precede him to the outer office.

Swanson followed them to his office door. "We'll notify the Brazilian authorities that we have Margaret

Turner in custody. I'll tell them where they can reach you for further information."

Apprehension clouded Terry's eyes and she hesitated. Had she remembered something important? Was there a reason she didn't want the Brazilian authorities involved? God only knew how truthful she'd been with him and the detectives.

Nevertheless, fool that he was, he put a hand to her lower back and urged her forward. They'd deal with the problem later when she'd rested, when his head and emotions weren't in so damn much turmoil.

The outer office was crowded with rows of desks, half of them manned with guys in rolled-up sleeves and loosened ties. Whether they were on the phone or sipping coffee, they all looked up as Terry passed by. Even with her hair a mess and her left eye beginning to bruise, she was hard not to notice.

The gentle and natural sway of her curvy hips was enough to draw anyone's attention. The fullness of her breasts was another head-turner, as was the way she carried herself—straight and tall with confidence. He had to remember that the physical package was deceiving.

When they got to the car, Terry stood at the passenger door without making an attempt to get in. "Would it be too presumptuous of me to ask for a ride?"

Anger and hurt and disappointment were all wrapped up in that one question. For a moment neither of them spoke, their gazes locked over the roof of the car. He was tempted to say yes, but he was beginning to recognize that stubborn tilt of her head.

She'd probably start walking and he'd end up feeling like a heel. Besides, her eye really was starting to look bad.

"Get in."

At his gruff command she lifted her chin.

"Please, get in." He yanked open his own door, annoyed that he somehow always gave in to her, and climbed behind the wheel.

She got in right away, but when he put the key in the ignition, she stopped him from starting the car by laying a cold hand over his. "Wait."

God, he hoped she didn't want to clear the air. Not now.

"We may have to go back inside. You'll have to tell me what you think I should do." She dug inside her jeans pocket and pulled out a fisted hand. She opened it, and two sparkling diamonds lay in the center of her palm. "I almost forgot about them."

He stared at the gems. He was no expert but they looked perfect, flawless...expensive. Looking up, he found her watching him with uncertainty, maybe even a little fear. "How the hell could you forget about those?"

She lifted a shoulder. "So much has happened..."

He leaned back and scrubbed at his face. Amazingly, he'd forgotten about them, too. She did things like that to him, damn it. "What do you want to do about them?"

"I don't know. Turn them over to the police? Wait and give them to the Brazilian authorities? What do you think is best?"

"Where were they all this time?"

"You had them."

Stunned, he drew his head back. "What?"

"The doll I left with Hope Katherine...these were the eyes. I substituted them for safekeeping. I hoped they wouldn't be noticed...until it was time."

Mitch thought back but he couldn't picture the porcelain doll. His laugh was short, full of irony. "You were right about that. Margaret didn't even notice them." He shook his head and lifted his gaze to Terry's weary face. "What did you mean, 'until it was time'?"

"I knew it was wrong to keep the diamonds, but I didn't even know I had them until I'd fled Rio. They were with the contents of my personal safe. I emptied it in a hurry when I left. I'd already been charged with smuggling. I wasn't about to turn the evidence over to the police without being able to defend myself." She took a deep breath. "I didn't know what would happen to me and I wanted to make sure Hope Katherine was well cared for."

The new information rocked Mitch off his foundation. He recalled the dingy efficiency where Terry had been living when she actually had the diamonds in her possession. She could have fenced them at any time, taken the vast amount of money the gems would have netted and lived a life of luxury somewhere in South America or Europe. But she'd left the diamonds for Hope.

He frowned, still amazed that they'd been sitting right under his nose. "How would anyone know what they were?" Doubt reared its head. Was she conning him? "I could have been careless with the doll and left it behind somewhere."

She shook her head without a trace of misgiving. "It's not the type of doll a child would play with. It's obviously an antique collectible. Anyway..." She looked a little sheepish as she sank back against the leather seat.

He smirked to himself. Here it came—the real reason why she'd left the diamonds with Hope.

She cleared her throat. "I was hoping you'd see them." A wistful uncertainty settled in the weariness around her eyes as she took a deep breath. "I thought that if you remembered our conversation that night in Rio, you'd—" she shrugged, looking sheepish again "—recognize the diamonds."

He frowned. "What conversation?"

The disappointment in her face made him feel as if he'd just flunked the most important test of his life.

"It was silly," she said, looking down at her hands. "It made sense at the time, but I was just...being foolish."

"Tell me which conversation."

She abruptly stuffed the diamonds back in her pocket and then wiped her palm on her jeans and stared out the passenger window. "You wanted me to take off my mask but I told you anything you needed to know about a person was in the eyes."

"I remember. You wouldn't take off the feather mask until we'd gotten in bed and turned off the lights. I thought you were being coy or mysterious."

Color blossomed in her cheeks. She probably remembered their incredible night of lovemaking just as he did with sudden and aching clarity.

"That wasn't my intention at all. My point was that you didn't need to see my face. You can tell a lot about person from their eyes. They're a reflection of their soul, of their values, of their entire being, and I knew that night, even before I needed you, that you were someone I could trust and count on."

The sincerity in her voice and face wasn't what softened him. His own recollection of their meeting was enough to give him pause. Their union had been almost spiritual, like nothing he'd ever experienced before. They'd bonded in a special way that night, in a way that was impossible to ignore.

Leaning his head back, he closed his eyes. "Do you know that it's been only a little over twenty-four hours since we met up again?"

"Seems like a year."

He snorted, but took no offense. He knew what she meant. "We have a lot of talking to do."

"I know." She wrapped her arms around herself in a protective gesture. "But right now, I'd really like to go see Hope Katherine."

Hope Katherine. Not just Katherine, or Hope.

"Yup. Me too." He started the car and pulled out of the parking lot into traffic. The entire way home he replayed what Terry had told Margaret about his inability to compromise. She was wrong.

Wasn't she?

"YOU'RE SUCH a big girl." Terry held Hope Katherine out in front of her, marveling at all the subtle changes that had taken place in the past few months. Her hair was still dark but starting to curl, and her eyes seemed lighter. More likely it was Terry's fuzzy memory. "Do you remember Mama, sweetie?"

Hope Katherine giggled and tried to grab Terry's hair. She'd always done that, and although Terry supposed all babies did, she chose to take it as a sign that Hope Katherine remembered her.

She hugged her daughter to her chest and breathed in her sweet baby smell. Lily had already fed and bathed her before they got home, and Hope Katherine really looked as though she wanted to sleep, but Terry couldn't help but hug and squeeze her, and assure herself that she was actually holding her baby again.

"She looks a lot like you." Lily stood at the nursery door smiling at them.

"Actually, she looks a lot like my sister Nina did as a baby. I can't wait for them to meet."

Before the words were out of her mouth, Mitch walked up behind Lily. No smile there. Terry turned back to Hope Katherine, trying not to read too much into his stern expression. She didn't fool herself that he would be willing to let her take their baby back to Rio. She simply didn't know what was going through his mind.

Earlier he'd sounded as if he'd been ready to throw her out in the street. At least now he seemed like he wanted to talk. They'd both been through a lot...too much...it was difficult to think straight.

"Okay, sweetie, I'll let you go to sleep," she said when Hope Katherine started to fuss in earnest. She couldn't resist giving her one last kiss on the cheek before settling her in her crib.

Lily and Mitch had already disappeared from the doorway and Terry took a final lingering look at her yawning daughter before joining them in the living room.

"You look totally beat," Lily said, shaking her head at Terry, and then glancing at Mitch. "You both do. I hope you plan on taking it easy."

Terry curled up on the sofa even though the other two were standing. She didn't know how much longer she'd last on her feet. "I am pretty tired."

"Well, if you don't need anything further, I guess I'll shove off." Lily looked at Mitch. "Unless you need a referee or something."

"Very funny, Bishop." His tone was wry, but he gave her a warm smile. "Thanks."

"Happy to oblige." She grinned back, then headed for the door. "You two take it easy. I'm serious." Before she let herself out, she added, "We need to talk tomorrow, Mitch. I know you've just been through a lot, but the information I have for you is pretty important."

He nodded, but Terry sensed his reluctance. More than reluctant, he seemed apprehensive, and she couldn't help but be curious. She didn't dare say a word, though. Enough tension radiated between them.

As soon as Lily closed the door behind her, Mitch took a seat on the leather recliner near the fireplace. He seemed in no hurry to talk, and Terry granted him silence. The truth was, she wasn't anxious to get into any heavy discussion, either. Not now when her head threatened to split open.

A throbbing pain had started near her left temple at the police station and had stayed with her in varying intensity throughout the evening. Not that she'd say a word about it to Mitch. He'd remind her that getting—as he would say—"conked" was her own fault, that she shouldn't have gone to see Meg on her own. No thanks. She didn't need that lecture, especially not now.

However, it did remind her of something...

"How are you feeling?" she asked, studying the way he let the weight of his head drop back against the headrest. It had been only yesterday that he'd suffered the same fate at the hands of Meg.

"With my fingers."

She frowned, not getting it at first, and then she smiled a little. "Ah, if you still have a sense of humor, it can't be so bad."

He sighed. "We have Hope back. Nothing seems so bad anymore."

"Nothing?"

She hadn't realized she'd spoken out loud until he looked sharply at her.

His probing gaze roamed her face until she wanted to curl up into a ball and pull a blanket over her head. "I hadn't planned on initiating any touchy discussions tonight."

"I don't want to, either," she agreed with a shudder. "I misspoke. I apologize."

He studied her a moment longer without speaking, and then asked, "How's your head?"

"Okay. How's yours?"

A reluctant smile curved one side of his mouth. "I've felt better, but I'll live."

She nodded. "I know what you mean."

"Hungry?"

"God, no." She automatically held her tummy, the thought of food making her nauseous.

"You haven't eaten all day. Maybe you should at least try to have some dry toast."

"Trust me, that would not be in my best interest right now. Or yours."

He half smiled again. "You couldn't deal me anything Hope hasn't."

She laughed softly. "That I understand too well. Nevertheless, I think I'll spare us both."

"How about hot tea?" He shrugged, an endearingly sheepish look crossing his face. "My mom used to make me tea. It seemed to help."

"A cup of hot tea sounds lovely. How about I make some for both of us?" She'd uncurled her legs and started to get up, but he was quicker.

He left the recliner and put his hands on her shoulders to keep her from standing. "Sit. I'll get the tea."

"But you aren't—"

"Terry?" The gruff affection with which he said her name silenced her. "Let me get your tea."

She quickly nodded, hoping he'd go and not see the tears beginning to well. Shrinking back, she curled up again, and he took his cue. As soon as he disappeared, she dabbed at her eyes.

Damn it, she'd been through too much in the past twenty-four hours, in the past year, to start getting emotional and daft now. His sudden kindness made her feel needy and hopeful, and she hated it.

But she didn't fool herself with this easier rapport they'd established in the past hour. He was still guarded and measuring, as if he no longer trusted her. She wondered, would he have done anything differently if he'd felt he had the power to get Hope Katherine released and involve no one else?

Or perhaps she'd jumped to a conclusion, and this new edgy attitude had something to do with more than his anger and disappointment that she'd met Meg alone. Maybe they were wrong to shelve any discussion. Maybe his whole attitude had nothing to do with her but something Lily had dug up for him.

One thing was for certain—she was making herself totally crazy guessing.

"I didn't know what kind of tea you wanted so I brought a selection." Mitch set a tray on the coffee table in front of her.

She stared up at him, amazed that he was back already.

"What's wrong?" Concern deepened his voice.

"Nothing. I was daydreaming and time slipped away."

"You didn't doze off?"

She frowned, confused at the odd remark. And then she remembered. "Oh, no, we're not going through that again."

He smiled as he stooped to pour the water for the tea. "Afraid so."

"You didn't get any rest last night. I did. You go on to bed. I doubt I could sleep anyway."

"You say that now." He offered her the tea selection. She chose Almond Sunset, and then he handed her a cup of steaming hot water. "You'll end up nodding off, though. You're too exhausted not to. Honey? Sugar?"

"No, thanks. Mitch?"

He picked up his own cup and looked at her with raised brows.

Terry immediately reconsidered what she'd been about to ask him. She'd been momentarily disarmed by his easygoing manner, but there was no invitation in his expression. He would not welcome a personal question.

"Never mind."

He frowned. "Go ahead, Terry."

She shrugged. "I lost my train of thought."

He didn't believe her. The way he pursed his lips and studied her told her that. But he didn't pursue the conversation. Instead, he returned to the recliner with his tea.

She took a long time dunking her tea bag, hating the uncomfortable silence that stretched between them. When had she become such a coward? Civil confrontation had never bothered her before. Clearing the air was always preferable to letting doubts and fears simmer to boiling.

She cleared her throat, set her cup on the coffee table. "I think I'll go look in on Hope Katherine."

"I just did while I waited for the water to boil. She's fine. Sound asleep with her pink teddy bear."

"Oh."

He sipped his tea, studied her over the rim of his cup. "You're going to have quite a shiner."

She frowned and shook her head, not understanding.

"That's another term for a black eye."

Her fingers automatically went to her cheek and she grimaced. "Great. I haven't seen my sister or anyone else in over a year and I'm going back to Rio looking like a boxer."

His expression fell. "So then I guess you're planning on returning right away."

The subtle indication that he didn't want her to go filled her with dangerous hope. "I don't know that I'll have a choice once the Brazilian authorities know I'm alive. And that I have the diamonds."

The reminder made her stiffen and she patted her pocket. Of course they were still there.

"You want to put them somewhere safe?"

She hesitated, a little surprised that he knew what she'd been thinking. Obviously her hesitation displeased him. He'd probably interpreted her reaction as reluctance because doubt and disappointment instantly darkened his face.

She dug into her pocket. "Yes. Absolutely. The last thing I need to do is lose them now." She met his measuring gaze. "That would sure shoot my credibility, wouldn't it?"

His left brow lifted.

"With the authorities."

He slowly nodded, but there was no mistake he got her double meaning.

She held out her hand, the twin diamonds glistening in the center of her palm. "Would you mind taking care of them?"

His gaze lowered to the gems, and then went back to her face. "If that's what you want."

"I do."

He set aside his cup and stood. She got up to meet him halfway. He waited, watching her, while she dropped the gems into their small red velvet pouch.

"Here." She handed them over without the slightest qualm. "I know you'll take care of them. Just like you did Hope Katherine." She swallowed. "Like you've taken care of me."

Regret haunted his eyes. "I'm sorry. I fell short there."

She gave her head an emphatic shake and pressed the pouch into his hand. "I expected too much."

"And I disappointed you."

"Oh, Mitch…" She clutched the front of his shirt and he put an arm around her, drawing her close.

"Shh." He kissed the tip of her nose, then drew back, his gaze roaming her face, lingering on her mouth.

Just as he lowered his head, his breath warming her lips, Hope Katherine let out a heart-wrenching wail.

CHAPTER FIFTEEN

MITCH WATCHED Terry lay Hope back in her crib. She'd gone back to sleep a half hour ago but Terry had continued rocking her gently and humming lullabies. He hadn't said anything, but just let her be. It had been a long time since she'd been able to hold Hope in her arms.

Just watching the two of them together made his insides go crazy. He didn't remember ever feeling so conflicted in his life. It was clear how much Terry loved their daughter. Not just the way she cuddled Hope or spoke of her, or the longing and pride that showed in Terry's face merely by watching their baby sleep.

She had sacrificed a great deal to keep Hope safe, her future secure. She'd even been willing to sacrifice herself. Having given him the diamonds earlier, she'd handed over far more than two priceless gems. She'd given away her freedom. He had to respect that kind of love and devotion, even if she didn't want him. Even if that knowledge hurt like hell.

Whatever kind of person Terry had once been, she was Hope's mother now…a damn good mother. She would clearly be a presence in their child's life, and he damn well better be prepared to accept that.

Bad enough he had to watch the beginning of his and Terry's end, but it looked as though there could be a new beginning for him—one he wasn't sure he wanted to embark on. Lily didn't have to tell him she'd found his father. He knew it from the look in her eyes. He knew it in his gut.

A month ago it would have been easy to nix a meeting if he got cold feet. Not now. Mitch had to consider that the man may not have had any knowledge of him, or like Terry, he'd had a solid reason to leave his son. Hard to fathom, yet Mitch had misjudged Terry quickly enough.

"Let's go."

Terry's low whisper took a few seconds to break into his preoccupation and she put a hand on his chest, urging him to move.

"I don't want to wake her," she added, an odd expression on her face, a mixture of curiosity and concern that made him think he must have inadvertently said something out loud.

He backed into the hall. She switched on the angel night-light and left the nursery door ajar.

He led the way into the living room, mentally kicking himself for wishing she'd touch him again. Tempted to share the couch with her, he returned to the recliner. "She remembers you."

"You think so?" Terry's eyes lit up. "I thought so, too. She sure smiles a lot now."

"She's smiling at *you*."

"Really?"

He nodded. "She's generally a little shy around strangers, so she definitely recognizes you."

"Shy? Who does she get that from?" Terry laughed, and then grimaced, her hand going to the side of her head.

"You okay?"

"Better than I've been in a long time." Her smile was faint before she yawned and grimaced again.

He felt so damn helpless. "Shall I put more water on for tea?"

"Not for me, thanks. But I think I'll take a nice warm bath."

"Not a good idea. It'll make you sleepy."

She stared at him with frustration, and then amusement. "I am thirty-one years old. I think I can decide whether I should take a bath or not."

"Thirty-one? Man, I didn't know you were *that* old."

She threw a cross-stitched pillow at him. He caught it and chuckled, relieved at the lighter mood they'd achieved.

"Tell you what, I'll skip the bath if you tell me what the deal is with Lily."

His mood plummeted. "There's nothing to tell."

"Mitch…"

"It has nothing to do with you."

"Whatever it is, it's bothering you and I want to help if I can."

"You can't."

"Oh, that's right, I forgot. You can take care of everything and everybody all by yourself."

He stared back at her, recalling the conversation she'd had with Margaret, his temper rising by the second.

She didn't back down. Her gaze remained level with his, daring him to lash out.

Damn it! She was the most annoying woman he'd ever met. How the hell had he ever been taken with her?

"Mitch, for God's sake, do you remember the things we told each other the night we met? No holds barred, as they say. I doubt you poured all that out just to get me into bed."

He wouldn't take the bait at first, and then he muttered, "You know better than that."

"So why won't you talk to me now?"

"There's nothing to talk about."

The stubborn glint in her eye told him she wasn't about to drop the subject. "It's about your father, isn't it? Did Lily find him?"

He matched her glare. "Don't you know when to back off?"

"Apparently not."

He sighed his frustration and rubbed his tired eyes. When he lowered his hands she was still staring at him. He muttered a curse. "I don't remember you being this obstinate."

"Oh, no, I've always been this way."

At the hint of amusement on her face, he snorted. "For someone who's on shaky ground you're awfully cocky."

She blinked, some of her bluster fading. But then she shrugged, and said softly, "I figure I have nothing to lose."

His chest tightened. Why? Because she planned on leaving soon? Because she knew they had no future.

Which meant he also had little to lose, except maybe his dignity.

He sighed. "It's about my father."

"She found him?"

"We didn't get to talk about the details yet, but that's my guess."

"Oh, Mitch, I'm so happy for you."

He grunted.

Her brows came down in a puzzled frown. "Isn't this what you wanted?"

"I don't want to talk about it now." He stood suddenly, his mind and body filled with restless energy.

"You never will."

The disappointment on her face and in her voice got to him. "Tell you what, after you take that nice warm bath you wanted, we'll talk all you want."

"Sure."

"I give you my word."

Her gaze narrowed. "What happened to your concern about me getting too drowsy?"

"That won't be a problem." He held out a hand to help her to her feet. "I'll be in there with you."

TERRY STEPPED gingerly into the tub full of warm sudsy water. Her skin tingled with anticipation of the soothing lavender-scented bath. Knowing Mitch would be joining her in another minute probably had something to do with it, too.

She was a fool to have agreed.

No hanky-panky, he'd said, he'd only be there to scrub her back, make sure she was okay.

Yeah, right.

She'd seen the desire in his eyes, felt the tightening in her breasts and belly.

Of course they could be mature adults about this, especially since they had Hope Katherine to consider. It was inevitable they would have to see each other in the future and it was important to preserve their relationship.

The knock at the door dispelled all rational thought. She sank lower into the water until the sudsy water covered her breasts. "Come in."

As soon as she saw the longing on his face, she knew the pretense was a joke. Heaven help her, she wondered what her own expression revealed.

He sat at the edge of the tub and trailed his fingers through the water. "Is it the right temperature?"

"Perfect."

"Need anything else?"

She shook her head. She meant it. Everything was perfect, and he'd done it all for her from filling the tub to selecting the relaxing lavender-scented bath salts. They probably had belonged to Meg, but Terry didn't care. She was too content to be here with Mitch and their daughter.

"Did you check on Hope Katherine?"

He smiled. "She's sound asleep."

Why was she so nervous all of a sudden? It wasn't as if he hadn't seen her naked before, not that he could see anything now. She took a deep breath. "I'm not going to fall asleep. In fact, I'm wide-awake if you have something else to do."

Mitch laughed. "Gee, let me see, maybe I should go load the dishwasher." He put a hand on her shoulder and started to massage a trail up her neck. "Yeah, that would be a lot more fun."

His voice had lowered, the huskiness of it sending a shiver down her spine. She dropped her head forward to allow him better access to her nape. He used his other hand to help rub deep into her tired, sore muscles.

"Hmm, you're a lot better nurse than I was."

"That's debatable." He massaged the base of her scalp. "I'll wash your hair if you want."

She closed her eyes. "Take your shirt off."

His hands momentarily stilled, and she could feel him staring at her.

She exhaled. "So you don't get it wet."

He didn't say anything, but she could imagine his smile, neither patronizing nor smug, but knowing and content. He kept the massage up another minute and then he withdrew, dried his hands and shrugged out of his shirt.

She let her head fall back so she could look at him, even though she remembered every detail of his muscled chest, the sprinkling of dark hair, the flatness of his belly. Although he had a terrific body, he wasn't one of those pretty-boy gym types who worked out so they could flex and primp. Mitch took pride in doing the best job he could, and that meant staying in top shape.

He took his time rearranging the thick royal-blue towels to accommodate his shirt, and then he hung it neatly on the rack, giving her an excellent view of his back and narrow waist. She wondered if she'd be pushing it to ask him to take off his pants.

She sank lower into the water until her chin barely cleared the surface. Was she ever looking for trouble. A jumble of totally inappropriate thoughts was giving her the headache from hell. Maybe that would cool her hot Latin blood.

"How about I light the candles, and we get rid of these bright lights?" He struck a match at the same time he asked the question.

"Fine." Her voice was a little high and for a moment she mourned the old Terry, the flamboyant, carefree young woman who wouldn't have given a second thought to teasing and taunting Mitch until he was eating out of her hand.

"Terry? I'll leave if you want."

She looked up to find him watching her, concern in his beautiful blue eyes. She shook her head. "I want you to join me."

He seemed startled, but pleased, perhaps a little uncertain.

"There's plenty of room. Besides, I owe you a massage."

His mouth lifted in a sexy grin. "How could I turn that down?"

"Come on, then." She patted the top of the water. When he didn't move quickly enough, she turned her hand over and flicked some water at him.

"Hey, you're getting cocky again." He unsnapped his jeans.

She held her breath. "And you love it."

He laughed, pulled down his zipper and shoved off his jeans. That left him in black silk boxers. And a bulge that made her breath swoosh out in a rush.

"Scoot up," he said, motioning with his chin.

"What?" She glanced behind her. What was he going to do?

He pulled off his boxers, and she swallowed. He was already hard but made no comment or apology about his aroused state. With a hand on her shoulder he urged her to slide forward, and then he lowered himself into the water behind her.

After spreading his legs, he drew her against him, her back leaning against his chest, his arousal nudging the top of her buttocks. Slowly he wrapped his arms around her and hugged her closer still, drawing his slick wet palms over her belly, down to her thighs and back up again.

She closed her eyes when he found her breasts. His arms crossed in front of her, he kneaded each breast with just the right amount of pressure to leave her breathless. Her already hard nipples tightened under his touch, and when he lightly pinched and rubbed, she couldn't stop the moan of longing from breaching her lips.

"Oh, Mitch..." She tried to twist around, to give as good as she got, but he wouldn't let her. His arms held her a willing prisoner as he kissed the side of her neck, nibbled her earlobe.

"Baby, be still," he said when she started to squirm again. "I told you nothing would happen and I meant it."

"This is nothing?" She didn't care that her voice was ragged, her chest beginning to heave. He knew what he was doing to her.

"I just want you to relax and feel good." He

picked up a bar of soap and glided it between her breasts. "Too much…uh…activity will make you hurt."

"Too late."

He froze. "Your head?"

She half laughed, half moaned. "My entire body."

"Damn it." He retreated. "I'm sorry."

"Not that kind of hurt." She guided his arms back around her, feeling a sudden self-consciousness that surprised her. "My body has changed since the pregnancy. Of course, you don't remember."

"I remember," he murmured, his lips against her neck. "You're still perfect."

He palmed one of her breasts and slid the soap over the other one. When he started to go down her belly, she sucked in a breath. He stopped short of the danger zone, the road of no return, as far as she was concerned. She wanted him to make love to her, but she wouldn't beg.

"You feeling okay?" he asked in a murmur near her ear.

"Looking for a compliment?"

He lightly bit her lobe. "That's not what I meant."

The tub was large, both deep and wide, one of the newer spa models, but not wide enough that she could turn around without his cooperation. As good as it felt to be stroked and caressed this way, she wanted to feel him under her palms, too. She wanted her breasts pressed against his hard chest.

"Mitch?"

"Shh… Lie back and close your eyes."

"This doesn't seem fair."

"To whom?"

She smiled, lowered her lids and got comfortable. "You're a nice man, Mitch Barnes, even when you try to pretend otherwise. Just don't blame me if I fall asleep."

"We can't have that." His hand slid down her belly again, and suddenly, dozing was the last thing on her mind.

"I take it back," she said with a gasp. "You aren't very nice at all."

MITCH GOT OUT of the tub first. The water had long since cooled and they were both so wrinkled it was a good thing only candles lit the room. Amazing how comfortable they could be with each other, yet in so many ways they still stumbled and fell when emotions ran high. Was it this way with all couples?

Hell, he didn't know. Sure, he'd had relationships before, but not like this, not this intense. The realization stopped him cold. It seemed impossible to feel this close to someone after such a short time.

His other relationships with women had been casual, sporadic, mostly due to his job. He was on the road most of the year. In fact, this was the first house he'd actually owned, and only because of Hope and the new job he was starting next week, which would keep him in one place.

"I thought you were going to pass me a towel."

Engrossed in his thoughts, he'd forgotten. He wrapped the towel he'd been using to dry himself around his waist, then pulled the second one off the rack. "Here it is."

Still under the cover of water and a few remaining suds, she put out a hand.

He smiled, shook his head. "Come and get it."

"Hey...you promised."

"I lied."

She gave him a dirty look.

"Terry, honey, I've already seen you naked."

She wrinkled her nose, crossed her arms over her chest. "Not postpregnancy."

It humbled him to realize she genuinely was disturbed by the changes in her body. This wasn't just a coy, teasing act.

Surely she didn't think that had anything to do with his reluctance to make love.

He smiled and opened up the towel for her. "Come on."

Uncertainty puckered her brows, but slowly she lifted herself and he kept his gaze on her face as she stepped out of the tub and into the towel. He wrapped it around her, and when she started to move away, he held her close and rubbed the plush terry down her back and arms, over her buttocks to her thighs.

He gave her a brief kiss, barely touching her lips with his. "Turn around."

Her eyes widened slightly and then she did as he asked.

She leaned into him, her back to his chest, as he rubbed her breasts and arms, then drew the towel down her belly. He wished like hell there was nothing separating them, that he could feel her warm skin against his, but this was better, he reminded himself.

He was having enough trouble keeping himself together.

"I think I'm dry," she said with laughter in her voice.

"You sure?" He took another swipe down her belly to her thighs.

She stiffened. "You're an evil man."

"And you love every minute of it."

"You're also impossible."

"That, too." He urged her to turn around to face him, which she did without hesitation.

When she tugged at the towel, he let it go and she wrapped it around her body. "Mitch, what's happening?"

His brows shot up, not sure he knew what she meant, not sure he wanted to know.

Annoyance flashed in her eyes, and then disappointment. "With us. Where do we stand?"

Unprepared for her bluntness and tenacity, he moved back and shoved a hand through his hair. "I don't know."

She lowered her lashes and brought the towel up to dab at the dampness around her neck and jaw. He didn't have to see her eyes to know he'd hurt her. Hell, what did she want him to say?

He didn't hear her claiming she wanted to stay, see if they could make a go of things.

"We have Hope to think about," he said. "This isn't just about the two of us anymore."

"I know that."

"Of course you do." He'd approached this all wrong.

"I meant that we'll have to see each other on a fairly regular basis, and I don't want to do anything that would jeopardize our relationship."

She blinked, pulled the towel tighter around her. "You mean joint custody."

He shifted uncomfortably. Why did she look so upset? Three days ago he thought hell would freeze over before he'd let her have anything to do with Hope. But things had changed. She was a good mother who'd acted out of desperation. "I think that's fair, don't you?"

She started to speak, stopped, and cleared her throat. "I guess so."

"You have another suggestion?"

She pressed her lips together and shook her head.

"Look, I seem to have upset you in some way. I'm sorry. I just didn't want you to think it's all about sex with us."

"I understand, really." She cleared her throat again. "I appreciate your being so—" she shrugged and caught her towel when it started to slip "—levelheaded about this."

No, she didn't. She was still upset. He saw it in her moist eyes, heard it in her unsteady voice. What did she think...that he would hand Hope back over to her? That he wouldn't want to be a major part of his child's life?

Yeah, well, she could think again.

CHAPTER SIXTEEN

THE NEXT MORNING Terry heard Mitch on the phone as soon as she left the guest room. It was still early, just after dawn, which made her think it was probably the police.

She thought about eavesdropping, but decided against it. She'd heard enough from him last night. He wanted Hope Katherine, but he didn't want her. Simple. Case closed.

So why should she be surprised, or disappointed, or anything else? He'd never promised her a thing. She knew he was a loner, in his late thirties, and hadn't even gotten close to marriage. It probably had something to do with his father's absence in his life, because whether Mitch knew it or not that bothered him a great deal.

It'd been clear that night of anonymity and masks and secrets in the dark. She thought of her own father and briefly closed her eyes. Parents had so much power over their children, she should be grateful Mitch was thinking about Hope Katherine and how their relationship would affect her.

In fact, Terry knew she should be relieved he wasn't going to fight her for full custody. No matter that she'd be cleared of all charges, he'd no doubt have an excellent chance of becoming the custodial parent, especially in an American court.

However, no amount of common sense or rationalization was going to shake her depression. She wanted what she couldn't have—to be a family. A normal family. She wanted Mitch to love her as much as she loved him.

The thought brought a warm flush to her entire body, and she briefly closed her eyes. She did love him, although she didn't know exactly when lust and respect had turned to love. Maybe it had happened when she realized what a great father he was. She had no idea, but it was there.

She smiled when she peeked into the nursery and saw that Hope Katherine was still sound asleep, her little mouth slightly open. It was such a joy to just look at her, and awfully tempting to go pick her up. But she needed to catch up on her rest. The last twenty-four hours had taken their toll.

Mitch hung up the phone as she walked into the kitchen, and he looked up with a tentative smile. Their parting had been on the abrupt side last night. "How's your head?"

"Much better. How's yours?"

He laughed, and the irony even made *her* smile. "Good. Want coffee?"

"At least a gallon."

He got down another mug, filled it with the dark brew, handed it to her and then refilled his. "Was the guest room comfortable enough?"

"Great." She averted his probing gaze. He'd wanted her to stay in his room last night. No hanky-panky, he'd promised. He was honest, she'd give him credit for that, but his rejection still hurt. "I hope you got some sleep."

"A couple of catnaps. I hope you didn't."

Her smile was wry. "Not likely." She'd thought about him all night, about how she knew he did care about her. He'd even checked in on her at least twice. So why couldn't they make it work? Why wasn't he willing to try? Could he not forgive her for leaving Hope Katherine? For going to meet Meg without him?

Her head still hurt at times, and she couldn't think altogether clearly. Plus she had a lot ahead of her to get straightened out before she could resume a normal life. She'd been forced to be patient for over a year now. She could wait a while longer.

"I just talked to Detective Swanson." Mitch paused until she gave him her attention. "Margaret gave them a full statement. He said it wasn't always coherent. Apparently she's really gone over the edge, but she was able to tell them enough to clear you and answer a lot of the Brazilian authorities' questions."

Terry should have been far happier, but sadness, a sense of loss weighed her heart. "Did she admit to the embezzlement?"

"Yeah, but she's fuzzy on the Swiss account she funneled the money to. Do you know a Peter Tirrell?"

"The name doesn't sound familiar."

"She hired him to dig up information on you and Hope at the Maitland Clinic in Austin. They have him in custody and he's also implicated her."

Terry took her coffee to the table and sat down. "I wondered how she knew about the baby or where I was."

"Apparently Meg found out that's where you had Hope. She hired Tirrell to break into your doctor's office, but that proved a dead end. Somehow her contacts in Rio knew about me because of Rick Singleton's investigation there. Margaret must have put two and two together and showed up here hoping to find you."

"But—" Terry shook her head, confused "—did she try to run Hope Katherine and me down that day? She wouldn't have known where to find me."

"That may have been an unrelated accident. If she mentioned it, Swanson didn't say anything." He picked up the coffeepot and lifted it questioningly. She shook her head and he refilled his own cup. "She admitted she'd been working with Leo Hayes. She'd promised him that with you out of the way, she could get him access to All That Glitters and help him expand his smuggling enterprise."

She sank back and exhaled. "I can barely believe all this. She was amazingly resourceful."

"*Obsessed* and *determined* would be better descriptions. And yeah, it is amazing what the human psyche allows us to do when a screw is loose. I've seen too much of it up close and personal."

Is that why he kept people at arm's length? She didn't dare ask. Not now. "How is Meg?"

"Physically, she's okay. The respiratory infection is responding to antibiotics and they removed the bullet and transferred her to the psychiatric ward. She'll be under guard until she can stand trial."

"I feel sorry for her."

"How can you possibly feel anything but contempt?" He stared at her, not with anger, but with a genuine curiosity. "She took our child, for God's sake."

"You said yourself, she's sick. She wanted to be loved. She wanted attention. She wanted to be wanted."

"Yeah, don't we all?"

The trace of caustic bitterness in his voice startled her. "Yes, but we aren't sick. We know how to cope when we don't get what we want."

"Cope? You mean, like run away?"

"What are you getting at?"

He sighed loudly. "I don't know. I shouldn't have said that."

Of course he was referring to that morning in Rio after they'd made love and she'd left without saying a word. It didn't seem to matter that it was a different time and they were different people then. Obviously he didn't know how to forgive or forget.

She sipped her coffee even though it was barely warm.

Silence stretched but she didn't care. She had nothing to say to him. Talking was useless. Mitch had his own plan that didn't include her.

"Why did you have me investigated?" he asked after a while.

"I already explained. I didn't hide what I did from you."

"Yeah, but I didn't realize you had me investigated before you had Hope."

"What does it matter? I only wanted to make sure you would be a decent father."

Oddly, he looked disappointed. "You're right. It doesn't matter."

But it did. She could tell by the way his expression fell. "Mitch, what's wrong?"

He snorted. "Nothing. Want some breakfast?"

"It's too early." She watched him walk to the window, look outside as if he were searching for something in particular. "Do the police want to talk to me again?"

"No, but I imagine the Brazilian police do." He started toward the door.

"Where are you going?"

He stopped, gazed down at her with sad eyes, then surprised her with a brief kiss on her forehead. "Just to get the paper."

She sat completely still until he disappeared out the door, wondering why that felt so much like a goodbye kiss.

MITCH LOOKED IN on Hope and then went to take a long warm shower. Not that he needed it. He wouldn't be surprised if parts of his skin were still wrinkled from last night. They'd spent an ungodly amount of time in the tub. But he hadn't wanted to give up the closeness, the physical contact they couldn't have had any other way.

God, she had no idea how noble he'd been last night. He'd come up with at least a hundred reasons why they should've made love, and only one why they shouldn't have. But that one was a doozy. Hope.

And if he was totally honest with himself, he didn't think he could handle it. If they had made love, he didn't know if he could gracefully let Terry go.

After his unsatisfying shower, he quickly dressed, checked once again on Hope, who, remarkably, still slept. It was early, though. Early enough that he was surprised to hear voices coming from the kitchen.

He'd made it halfway down the hall when he realized it was only Terry's voice and she was on the phone. Who the hell would she be talking to this early? He stopped short of the door and listened.

"I've missed you, too," she was saying. "But it's over. Meg confessed. Have the authorities there contacted you?"

After a pause she said, "But I don't have a passport, and neither does Hope Katherine."

Mitch tried to remain calm and not jump to conclusions.

Terry wouldn't take their baby without his consent.

"Nina, are you sure?"

God, he was tempted to pick up the extension. He wouldn't, though. When she got off the phone, he'd ask her what was happening and she'd tell him.

"If that's the case, then I suppose I could get a flight out tonight. I called the airlines earlier, and there's one to Rio at nine, San Antonio time."

Mitch felt the blow as if it had been dealt with a sledgehammer. She couldn't wait to leave him, get back to the comfort of her old life. How could he be such a fool over and over again? Here he'd just been thinking that they had a little time to get used to one another under normal circumstances. That maybe since the stress was removed they'd find common ground.

Hell, she'd already called the airlines.

He didn't bother cowering outside the door anymore. He walked into the kitchen and headed for the coffeepot.

She didn't jump or look guilty or even seem to mind he was there. In fact, she gave him a tiny smile. He didn't know why, but it irritated the hell out of him.

"I'm not sure, Nina," she said, turning back to the phone. "Everything has happened so fast. But as soon as I know I'll call you back." She paused and listened. "No, you've done enough. I'm fine, really—"

She broke off when her voice cracked.

Mitch finished filling his mug and replaced the coffeepot, his heart thudding. He slid her a glance. She looked as though she was fighting back tears.

She said something briefly in her own language, and then hung up.

He busied himself with rinsing the empty coffeepot to give her some privacy.

She sniffed, then cleared her throat. "That was my sister. I made the call to her and of course I'll pay for it."

"I don't care about that."

"No, I'm sure you don't…." She paced to the window, shoving her hands through her hair. She looked nervous, edgy. "The Brazilian authorities are working on getting me traveling papers. They want me back as soon as possible so they're cutting red tape to do it."

"I'm sure you want to get back as soon as possible yourself." His gaze stayed level with hers until she looked away.

She shrugged. "I miss Nina."

"Did I hear you say something about a flight tonight?" he asked casually.

She nodded. "Unless there's a reason I should stay here longer."

His thoughts scattered. He should tell her to stay because he needed and wanted her. What did he have to lose? His pride? "What about Hope?"

"I don't suppose you'd let her come with me?"

"What do you think?"

She sighed. "I wouldn't want to put her through the trauma, anyway. She's better off here until I get everything straightened out with the authorities back home. I don't want any question as to my innocence."

"And then?"

She crossed her arms over her chest and hugged herself. "I guess we need to discuss that, don't we?"

The phone rang, startling them both.

Mitch snatched it up before it woke Hope.

It was Lily.

He glanced at the clock—only eight-fifteen. He hoped she wasn't going to start in on him meeting with his father again. Not now. "What are you doing calling so early?"

"Early? I've already been to the office. Anyway, I

knew you'd be up. Can I come over? I'll bring dough-nuts.''

"Now is not a good time."

She hesitated. "Look, I have to go to Dallas at eleven and I won't be back for a couple of days. What I have to tell you can't wait that long."

Now she had him worried and curious. He glanced at Terry. She stared out the window, a faraway look on her face, probably already planning her arrival home.

He swore to himself. When stuff happened, it came in waves.

"All right, come over. But I'm not making any promises."

Terry turned and looked at him then, watched as he hung up the phone and went back to washing the coffeepot. He knew she was waiting for him to fill her in. He might as well. As soon as Lily arrived, it wouldn't be a secret.

"Was that Lily?" she asked.

"Yeah." He frowned. "How did you know?"

"About your father?"

"I don't know what it's about."

Her lips curved in a knowing smile. "Meet with him, Mitch. Give him a chance."

"A chance for what? To explain why he left my mom?"

"That, and a chance to show you that he just might be a decent human being worth knowing."

"I have enough on my plate with taking care of Hope."

That shut her up for a moment. She drew in her

lower lip and took a deep breath. "If she has a grandfather, she deserves to know him."

"Yeah, and what if he's a no-good bum?"

"What if he's not?"

"This isn't your business, Terry." He threw down the dish towel and walked out of the kitchen.

She followed him. "Mitch, please don't do anything you'll regret."

He kept walking and ignored her. She had a lot of nerve lecturing him. Her choices hadn't exactly made life a bed of roses. One night, and she thought she knew him. Women. Why didn't they know when to mind their own damn business? Lily was just as bad. Good thing he'd never gotten married.

When he entered his bedroom, he figured she'd back off. He was wrong. She stayed on his heels.

"Do you mind?" He turned and glared. "I have things to do in here."

"Yes, I do. You're going to listen to me. Whether you like it or not, I care about you, and I don't want you to do anything rash just because you're stressed out over Hope Katherine and me."

"This has nothing to do with you."

She put her hands on her hips. "Oh, that's right, tough guy, I forgot. Nothing has anything to do with anybody for you. Mitch Barnes handles everything by himself. He acts alone. He needs no one."

He moved closer but she didn't budge an inch. "Okay, you want to go there? I wasn't going to bring it up but I heard what you told Margaret."

A puzzled frown drew her brows together.

"About how I'm a loner, how I don't know how to compromise."

"And?"

Her lack of reaction took him aback. "That's a bunch of garbage."

"No, it's not. It's the truth, and if you'd stop and think about it for a moment you'd see that."

"You don't know what you're talking about."

"You don't even like having a job that requires a partner. That's why you liked your position with the Bureau. Most of the time you work alone, you live alone. Frankly I'm surprised you're willing to take on the care of an infant. At some level it requires you to depend on someone."

He smiled. "Oh, I see, you're trying to convince me to hand over Hope. Forget it."

She startled him by slapping his arm. Not hard, but it got his attention. "You jackass. I'm talking about you, not our daughter, not us. I don't want you to pass up an opportunity. Yes, your father is a stranger to you, but when you were forced into it, you asked a stranger to help save your child, the most precious thing in your life.

"Neither one of us knew that cab driver but we both had to count on him. And guess what? He came to the rescue. He went above and beyond. Give people the benefit of the doubt, and you might find they'll live up to your expectations."

He didn't know what to say. He didn't agree with her, but the earnestness in her eyes tempered his annoyance. She'd said she cared about him, and he believed her. But how much? Enough to stick around and explore their relationship?

She didn't move, didn't even look away. She stared back, waiting for him to respond, weariness shadowing the skin below her eyes, yet she was concerned enough to stand up to him. Foolish as it might be, it gave him hope.

"I have a question for you."

She blinked. "Okay."

"When you were talking to Margaret, and she asked you what you would do if she let you and Hope go, you told her you didn't know."

Her forehead creased in thought. "I don't remember that...."

No way she wouldn't remember. She simply didn't want to answer. Except she looked genuinely confused.

She shrugged.

"Margaret pointedly asked you if you would take Hope and run, or come back to me."

Terry frowned. "Oh, I vaguely remember now. I told her I didn't know because I wasn't sure what she was getting at. I figured she had a 'right' answer in mind. I just didn't know which one it was and I didn't want to incite her."

The explanation was so simple, so obvious he shook his head and laughed.

"Mitch? What's wrong?"

He scrubbed at his face. "Nothing. I just— Nothing's wrong."

She narrowed her gaze with misgiving. "You need more rest."

"You're right. When Lily gets here, tell her to go away."

Clearly she found no humor in his feeble joke. Annoyance joined the weariness in her features. "You're a coward."

He sighed and turned away. "I don't need you butting in. I've got everything under control."

"Really? Then I suggest you fix your shirt." That said, she walked out of the room.

Mitch frowned and looked down.

His shirt was inside out.

CHAPTER SEVENTEEN

TERRY HAD JUST finished changing Hope Katherine's diaper when the doorbell rang. Good. She hoped Mitch and Lily ended up at the kitchen table because then Terry had the perfect excuse to eavesdrop.

She sat in the rocking chair near the pink toy box with Hope Katherine in her lap. "What do you say, sweetie? Shall we give your daddy some time to dig himself a hole before we go butt in?"

Her eyes wide, Hope Katherine watched Terry slip on her red-and-white booties. She giggled when Terry hit a ticklish spot in the arch of her foot.

"Oh, what was that?" Terry laughed and dragged her finger across the spot.

Hope Katherine howled and threw her head back. She was strong enough that her entire body lurched backward. Terry's heart raced as she flung her arms around her daughter's sturdy little body to keep her from tumbling over.

"Hey, missy, looks like I'm going to have to get in shape to keep up with you."

Hope Katherine giggled and reached up to tangle her fingers in her mother's hair. It was almost inconceivable to Terry that she'd be separated from her baby again, even if just for a week. It was tempting to put off going back to Rio, but the sooner she cleared herself, the sooner she could get on with her life.

But what kind of life would it be?

An empty one without Mitch.

She knew now he wouldn't be unreasonable about sharing custody. She'd keep an apartment here in San Antonio in order to see Hope Katherine regularly. Though she didn't fool herself that it wouldn't hurt like hell to see Mitch.

If he'd only ask her to stay. No promises or guarantees, just for a trial—just to see if they were compatible for the long haul. She wouldn't be the one to bring it up, though. If she did, she doubted Mitch would rebuff the suggestion. But only for Hope Katherine's sake.

That wasn't enough for Terry. She'd stay only if Mitch wanted her, if he said he loved her. The truly odd thing was, she believed he did love her. As best he knew how. But there would always be that invisible barrier he kept erected between himself and anyone else who tried to get close.

Maybe that was a common symptom of a person who'd felt abandoned by a parent. She had no idea. She only knew that until Mitch chose to let down his guard a bit, they didn't have a chance. As for Hope Katherine, in the end, no child was content with parents who tried to fake happiness.

"Well, kiddo, what do you think?" Terry held Hope Katherine in the air and let her kick her feet. Gosh, she was heavy—almost as heavy as Terry's confused heart. "Are you ready? Let's go see Daddy."

"DO YOU KNOW who he is?" Mitch asked as he calmly poured Lily a cup of coffee.

"Not for sure. But I have a strong suspicion."

She probably expected him to ask who she thought his father was, but Mitch wasn't ready. He might have been if Lily hadn't seemed so nervous herself. On the surface she looked fine, but he'd gotten to know her well over the past few months. She was as close a friend as any woman had ever been to him, and he knew instinctively something was wrong.

Yet he'd never known her to hold back on him before. In fact, she often told him more than he wanted to hear.

"Am I going to be shocked? Pleasantly surprised? Angry?"

She fiddled with her mug and ignored the doughnuts she'd brought. "I don't know. Pleasantly surprised, I think."

"Why the rush all of a sudden?"

"If I'm right, I think he's going to make himself known to you. I wanted to prepare you if that's the case." She got up, went to the sink and rinsed out her mug. "Like I told you earlier, I have to go to Dallas today, and I'll be gone a few days."

Mitch stared at her but she wouldn't look at him. "Who is he, Lily?"

"I'd rather not say—I have to give him the chance to come forward."

Mitch wasn't sure how he felt about that cryptic

answer, or the guarded expression on her face. Maybe he was just being touchy. He still smarted over his conversation with Terry, and for all he knew, she was all packed and ready to go by now.

What would he do tomorrow when he woke up and realized she was thousands of miles away, when she should be waking up beside him? What would she say if he asked her to stay? She'd agree, he figured, but only so that she could be near Hope. Not him. Could he be content to accept those terms?

Mitch thought about his father, imagining how he'd feel himself if he'd never had the opportunity to be a part of Hope's life. "What's he like?"

The guarded look returned to Lily's face, making him want to reconsider his decision.

"Never mind," he said. "I'll find out soon enough for myself."

She blinked. "So you will agree to meet with him then?"

"That's what I said." He hadn't, exactly. But she ignored that and his gruff tone.

Rising and launching herself across the table, she threw her arms around his neck. "Oh, Mitch, you won't be sorry."

"I don't know. I may be already." He drew back to stare into her misty eyes. "What's going on?"

She shrugged. "Reunions always make me sappy. You know that."

"Aren't you being a little premature?"

She smiled and picked up her purse. "I'd better get to Dallas."

"Lily?"

She'd already made it to the door, but she stopped and turned, her expression slipping into caution mode. "Mitch, please, you'll just have to trust me."

He shook his head. "It's not about— Never mind. Go, before the traffic gets bad."

Her gaze narrowed and she took a step back toward him. "What is it? What's wrong?"

"Nothing. We'll talk when you get back."

"Is it about Terry?"

Mitch laughed to himself. When was he ever going to learn? Women. They just couldn't leave things alone. He stretched out a kink in the side of his neck. The thing was, he did want Lily's perspective.

"I have a question for you," he said finally, "and I want an honest answer."

"Shoot."

"Do you consider me a loner?"

"Yup."

"Uncompromising?"

A knowing grin lifted the corners of her mouth. "Sometimes…okay, often."

"In what ways?"

"Wait." She came back to the table and set her purse down, and he cringed inwardly. Hell, he'd asked for this. "I have a question for you."

"Yeah?"

"Maybe even a couple." She grinned when he sighed. "Have you been enjoying your role as father?"

Indignation shot up his spine. "You know I have."

"Why haven't you ever gotten married? Started a family?"

"This coming from you?" He snorted. "You worked for the Bureau. You know what it was like. Not exactly conducive to family life."

Her eyebrows rose in a patronizing expression. "Weren't any of the other agents you worked with married?"

"Come on, Lily. You know what I mean."

"Well, were they?"

"Of course."

"Any of them happily married?"

Mitch grunted. What had he expected? "All right, you made your point."

Lily stared at him, concern and compassion in her eyes. "Have I?" She gave him a light punch in the arm. "I sure hope so. Not just for your sake, but for Terry's and Hope's."

"Hope Katherine," he muttered, his thoughts starting to form a whirlpool of confusion in his head.

Lily picked up her purse again. "Hope Katherine? Is that her middle name?"

He shrugged. "We call her that now. Terry had named her Katherine. Using both names seems fair."

"I like it."

He shrugged again, but couldn't keep a smile from tugging at his mouth. "Yeah, it kind of grows on you."

Lily laughed. "Okay, now I've really got to go." She hesitated before opening the door. "Mitch, the Bureau taught you to use your head and your gut. This time, listen to your heart."

He said nothing as he watched her close the door behind her. He didn't know how long he'd been staring out the window when he heard Hope Katherine gurgle. Looking behind him, he found Terry standing in the hall near the door, holding their daughter.

God only knew how long they'd been standing there, or how much Terry had heard. At this point, he guessed it didn't matter. She'd be gone soon.

The thought had as much impact as a physical blow and he exhaled sharply. "I see Sleeping Beauty finally decided to wake up."

"Yes, and she's hungry." Terry's smile and pleasant disposition did nothing to boost his spirits. Obviously she was happy about leaving.

"I'll heat something up for her."

"Mitch?"

He'd already opened the refrigerator, and something in her tone made him want to avoid her eyes. He forced himself to close the door and turn to her. The expression on her face took the starch out of him. Was it regret, desperation?

She smiled again, a bit shyly this time. "I know it's none of my business, but did Lily come about your search for your father?" She sighed loudly before he could answer. "Never mind. I heard. I won't pretend I didn't, and I think it's wonderful you've agreed to meet him."

He shrugged. At least one of them was enthusiastic. "I have to know. I need—" His thoughts scattered.

"You need closure, either way."

"I suppose." The intensity in her gaze started to unnerve him. She obviously had something else to say. But so did he.

"Look, about you going back to Rio..."

Caution entered her eyes, and something else. Surprise? Hope, perhaps? Or was that wishful thinking on his part?

"Yes?" she prodded when he'd trailed off.

"I've been giving it some thought." He rubbed the back of his neck, broke away from her probing gaze, went back to rooting around in the refrigerator. Hope Katherine was hungry, after all.

"Mitch?" Impatience barbed her voice. "What?"

He brought out some applesauce. "If you want to take Hope Katherine back with you so your sister can see her…well, it's okay."

When his offer met with silence, he looked at her. Disappointment clouded her face as she sank to a chair with the baby on her lap.

What the hell? He thought she'd be pleased. "Look," he added, "if you're worried about the passport issue, I could probably pull some strings. But it'll take a day or two."

"That's wonderful. Nina will be happy to finally see her niece." Her face and tone were expressionless, igniting his irritation.

"If you don't want to make the trip back, I'll come and get her in about two weeks." He busied himself with dishing up Hope Katherine's applesauce.

"Fine. Great. Thank you."

He cleared his throat. "I'll make the call."

She frowned. "What call?"

"To get Hope Katherine's traveling papers."

"Oh, right." Her smile lacked enthusiasm.

He put the applesauce in the microwave, set it at half power, and then went to the phone. He picked it up, punched in three numbers and then slammed the receiver back down.

Terry and Hope Katherine both jumped.

Without a word, he lifted his daughter out of Terry's arms and placed her in her highchair. Terry's mouth opened in surprise, her eyes widening when he took her hands and pulled her to her feet.

"I have something else to say." He slid his arms around her. "In a minute," he added before lowering his lips to hers.

She didn't hesitate to circle her arms around his neck as she accepted the kiss. More than merely accepting, she was an eager participant, opening her mouth to him, tasting his passion, giving some of her own.

He was the one who pulled away first. "Terry, you can't do this."

She blinked, a little dazed, and stared at him in frustrated confusion. Wasn't he the one who started this business?

"You can't go back to Rio without giving us a chance."

Terry frowned, and then as comprehension started to sink in, her pulse speeded up. "Because of Hope Katherine?" she asked cautiously.

"No." He looked directly into her eyes, and there was no mistaking his meaning. "Because we're good together. Because I need you." He took a deep and endearing breath. "Because I love you."

A sob caught in her throat. That's all she needed to hear. "I love you," she whispered. "I have from the beginning."

He hugged her tighter. "We'll make it work."

"You already have." When he pulled back, she met his puzzled look with a mysterious smile. In her heart she'd known everything would be all right as soon as she'd overheard him use Hope Katherine's name.

"If you want me to go back to Rio with you, I'm sure I can find some kind of work there."

"What about the new job you're starting next week?"

He smiled and gently dragged the back of his hand down her cheek. "Honey, I can always find a job. Where would I find someone like you and Hope Katherine?"

Giddiness filled her. He was really trying. "We'll stay here. Nina and Rick were only in Rio for my sake—they want to make their home in the States. And you have family here in San Antonio, too."

Mitch frowned.

"Lily," she said simply. "She's family."

He blinked. "Yeah, I guess she is." And then he smiled and pulled her to him again. "How did I ever get so lucky?"

EPILOGUE

Double G Ranch, One month later

"GLAD YOU COULD MAKE IT." Lily walked toward Mitch and Terry and Hope Katherine, six-month-old Elizabeth perched on her hip. Behind her, near the garages, a family basketball game was in progress. "Although you may be sorry. Must be a full moon. Everyone's in rare form."

"So what's new?" Mitch gave her a grin when she made a face, and then switched his attention to Elizabeth. He wasn't sure why Lily had included them in the Garretts' family reunion, but he was touched that she had. Terry was right. He did consider Lily and her brother and sister family.

Lily had taught him so much about being a father and husband...almost husband. He and Terry had decided to make the announcement today.

Elizabeth cooed and her mother's smile broadened as she touched the baby's cheek. "Hey, haven't you had enough attention from everyone today?"

Hope Katherine put in her nonsensical two cents and everyone laughed.

"There's not enough attention in the entire universe for these little tykes," Terry said, and glanced at Mitch. "Especially when their daddies spoil them."

"What?" Mitch reared his head back. "Not me."

"Of course not." Terry and Lily exchanged knowing smiles.

"Hey, it's about time you got here," Dylan called out as he held a basketball over his wife Julie's head. "We need help. The women are creaming us."

Julie surprised him by jumping up and knocking the basketball out of his hand. It rolled toward Ashley, who stood on the sidelines, but her very pregnant belly prevented her from scooping it up in time.

Her husband, Kyle, got it for her.

"Traitor," Dylan yelled, and Julie smacked him playfully on the arm.

Lily sighed and looked at Mitch with a long-suffering expression. "It's not too late to make a run for it."

Her husband, Cole, joined them at that moment. "She's full of it. You couldn't pry this woman away from her family with the Jaws of Life." He offered Mitch his hand. "Good to see you." He kissed Terry on her cheek, and gave Hope Katherine's a tweak, which never failed to make her giggle.

His gaze met Mitch's. "William asked if you'd go see him in his den."

Out of the corner of his eye, Mitch saw Lily straighten. Cole gave her an affectionate wink. "Sure." Mitch turned to Terry, his heart beginning to slam against his chest. He knew what this was about. Deep down in his gut, he knew.

"Go ahead," Cole said, grinning and slipping an

arm around each of the women's shoulders. "I'll take care of the ladies."

"Good." Lily gave him Elizabeth. "One of them needs her diaper changed."

Mitch laughed along with Terry, but his mind was on the man in the big house. Terry made a shooing motion with her hand, and he headed toward the backdoor.

William Garrett was seated at his desk when Mitch walked into the den, but the older man immediately got up, his smile uncharacteristically tentative. "Thanks for coming, Mitch."

"Are you kidding? Would I miss a Garrett shindig?"

William seemed to relax. "I won't beat around the bush. As it is, what I have to say isn't going to be easy. You'd better have a seat."

Mitch didn't argue. He knew for sure what this was about now. Every nerve in his body reacted with a sixth sense. He took a seat across from William and remained silent.

William cleared his throat. "I understand you've been looking for your father."

He nodded, and waited while William fidgeted with his collar.

"Hell, there's no easy way around this, so I'm going to speak plain." His eyes bore into Mitch's. "I'm the man you're looking for." When Mitch sat frozen, William took a deep breath, his broad chest heaving with the effort. "I hope you're as pleased as I am."

For a moment, Mitch was unable to speak. Even

though he knew this was coming, emotion overwhelmed him.

"I didn't know about you," William continued. "It's important to me that you believe that. Your mother was a fine woman, and she helped me out at a time when I was feeling lost after my own father's death. I'll always thank Bobby Jo for that."

Still numb, Mitch found he couldn't speak.

"I've known for a couple of months now—I had a DNA check done myself once Dylan had you sign a medical release for the search. But you had enough in your life to deal with, what with Hope and Terry." William's blue eyes glistened. "I have to tell you, Mitch, I couldn't be more pleased to have you as a son."

The older man's words wrapped themselves around Mitch like a warm comforting blanket. "My father…"

His voice was barely audible, and William seemed unsure, but then he rose from his chair and walked around the desk. Mitch stood, and William embraced him.

"Welcome to the family," William whispered, his voice thick with emotion.

"I couldn't have found a better one." Mitch stared into the older man's face and wondered if his own eyes were as misty as William's.

"You can come in now," William called out unexpectedly, and the door immediately opened.

Mitch turned to find Lily standing there, her eyes shining.

William laughed. "I knew you couldn't wait."

Indignation flashed. "Me?"

Dylan moved in behind her and smiled at Mitch. "Welcome, Bro."

"Hey," was all Mitch could manage to reply.

Lily sighed and then rushed him for a hug. "You wouldn't be in the market for another job, would you? It just so happens Finders Keepers is looking."

Dylan patted his sister's arm and shook his head. "Impatience sure does run in the family."

Mitch smiled. So did love and understanding. He was lucky to become a part of the Garrett clan.

Terry came to the door, looking confused and concerned, and he motioned her inside. He slipped an arm around her and held her close. In fact, he was the luckiest man in the world.

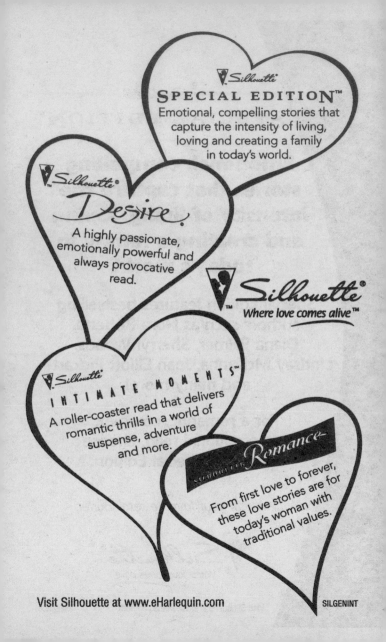